"Who says we're playing by your rules?"

Daniel demanded, his anger returning. "Loosen up a bit, will you, Abby? What are you so scared of, anyway? That I might want more than a small kiss?"

No one had ever talked to her that way.

"You're in no danger from me," Daniel continued. "I never mix business with pleasure. A beautiful woman deserves as much attention as a business venture. Careful evaluation of her needs, deciding the most effective mode of operation, figuring in advance how to maximize potential can all be applied as effectively to a date as to a business project."

Abby stared at the road. The man was dangerous, and she wanted him out of her life. Now.

The comparison she'd made the first day had been right. Daniel Hawthorn was a shark, and she was a guppy. Challenging him had been her biggest mistake. She was out of her league, out of her depth—and *out of her mind*.

Dear Reader,

It's a brand-new year, and we at Silhouette Romance have a brand-new lineup of dashing heroes, winsome heroines and happy endings galore! Winter is the perfect season to curl up and read—you provide the hot cocoa, and we'll provide the good books!

We're proud to launch our new FABULOUS FATHERS series this month with Diana Palmer's *Emmett*. Each month, we'll feature a different hero in a heartwarming story about fatherhood. *Emmett* is a special book from a favorite author in more ways than one—it's Diana Palmer's fiftieth Silhouette novel, and it's part of the LONG, TALL TEXANS series, too!

This month, Stella Bagwell's HEARTLAND HOLIDAYS trilogy is completed with *New Year's Baby*. It's a truly emotional tale that brings the Gallagher clan's story to a satisfying conclusion.

Rounding out the month, we have Geeta Kingsley's *The Old-Fashioned Way,* Carolyn Monroe's *A Lovin' Spoonful,* Jude Randal's *Northern Manhunt,* and an inspiring romance from first-time Silhouette author Jeanne Rose, entitled *Believing in Angels.*

In the months to come, watch for Silhouette Romance titles by many of your favorite authors, including Annette Broadrick, Elizabeth August and Marie Ferrarella.

Here's to a sparkling New Year!

Anne Canadeo
Senior Editor
Silhouette Romance

THE
OLD-FASHIONED WAY
Geeta Kingsley

Silhouette
V™ **R O M A N C E**™
Published by Silhouette Books New York
America's Publisher of Contemporary Romance

For my mother, whose spirit is forever young

SILHOUETTE BOOKS
300 E. 42nd St., New York, N.Y. 10017

THE OLD-FASHIONED WAY

ISBN: 0-373-08911-2

First Silhouette Books printing January 1993

Books by Geeta Kingsley

Silhouette Romance

Faith, Hope and Love #726
Project Valentine #775
Tender Trucker #894
The Old-Fashioned Way #911

GEETA KINGSLEY

is a former elementary school teacher who loves traveling, music, needlework and gardening. Raised in an army family, she was never lonely as long as she had books to read. She now lives in Southern California with her husband, two teenagers and the family dog. Her first published novel, *Faith, Hope and Love,* was a finalist in the Romance Writers of America's RITA competition.

Geeta believes in the triumph of the human spirit, and this, along with her concern for the environment, is reflected in her characters and stories.

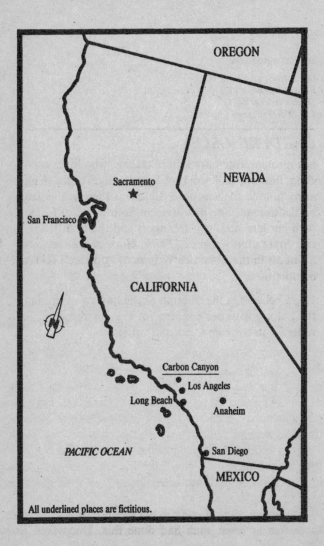

OREGON

NEVADA

Sacramento ★

San Francisco

CALIFORNIA

Carbon Canyon

Los Angeles

Long Beach

Anaheim

PACIFIC OCEAN

San Diego

MEXICO

All underlined places are fictitious.

Chapter One

Abby swallowed hard as her gaze tangled with the speaker's. She shouldn't have chosen a seat in the front row. Shouldn't have placed herself within range of the powerful magnetism he exuded. Her mind flashed a warning. She had long ago vowed to stay away from men like Daniel Hawthorn. Forever.

Telling herself it was the artist in her that took note of every detail of him was a lie. This feeling was primal. It was the woman, not the artist, that noticed everything. Confidence that could be scooped up with a shovel, sexy eyes, potent charm. Added to his looks it spelled an attraction that was intense, dangerous, *mind numbing*.

Every action of his produced a reaction. The deep baritone voice strummed a chord deep in her heart. He lifted a brow and her pulses thrummed. Every time their gazes met, her skin tingled.

The ebb and flow of color in her face confirmed the truth. Awareness at fever pitch had done this. Uncovered emotions Abby never wanted exposed again. Tuning in to the man on a personal level spelled danger. For her.

She shouldn't have come.

Daniel Hawthorn's seminar, How to Help an Ailing Business, wasn't going to help her, or Gran. As for the man's charm, she could do without it.

Rod, her late husband, had been charming and a glib talker, too. And so cold. Unfortunately Abby hadn't discovered that before they were married. Blinded by her feelings, she hadn't seen the warning signs till it was too late.

Thinking of the past was like poking her fingers into an electric socket . . . the shock jarred Abby back to the reason she was here.

Gran. The dearest person in the world. Abby's rock. She owed her more than could be repaid in one lifetime. Gran had raised her, been there for her whenever she needed her. Now their roles were reversed. Gran needed her help. Only, Abby was making as much headway as a butterfly trapped in a net.

The Busy Bee, the craft store they owned jointly with two others, wasn't doing well. The bank manager's warning still rang in Abby's ears. They had a month to pull the store out of the red, or the bank would be forced to foreclose on its loan.

Fear gripped Abby. The Busy Bee was Gran's lifeline. It gave her a reason to get up in the mornings, an interest in life. There had to be a way of saving it.

She looked at Daniel Hawthorn. Thoughts of Gran and the store had fueled the worry inside her into a blaze. The man had no right to have this effect on her. Sparks of anger sent heat through her. The advertisement she had seen in a leading business magazine had boasted that Daniel Hawthorn was a genie when it came to helping any business in trouble. So far his magic hadn't worked for her. Nothing he had said could be applied to The Busy Bee.

Abby's eyes narrowed at the thought of the money she had spent on this seminar. The *last* of her money. Pictures whirled in her brain. Mr. Hawkins, the bank manager, refusing to extend them any more credit. Gran's face, pinched with the worry that she always tried to hide. Gran's friends, wondering what would happen to them when The Busy Bee closed. Worry pumped adrenaline into Abby's bloodstream. She had to do something. Right now.

Daniel's gaze went back to the woman in the first row. Now, as all through the day, the green eyes regarded him seriously. The mass of black wavy hair that bordered a wide forehead was raked back by long slim fingers. His gaze rested on the tumble of hair on her shoulders. The realization that he wanted to touch it shook him.

The feeling was an unfamiliar one. She wasn't the sophisticated, every-hair-in-place type that normally attracted him.

It had become a habit of Daniel's to classify the people attending these seminars into successes and failures. She belonged in the latter category. She didn't take notes or ask any questions. Her desperate look had remained fixed on him as if she hoped the process of osmosis would transfer all he knew to her. Instinct honed during years of conducting these seminars told him she absorbed very little of what he said. She was worried.

It's really none of your business, Hawthorn.

Daniel forced himself to look away, unclench the hand in his pocket. He had a personal rule not to get involved with anyone in the audience. Yet the woman drew him like a magnet. Maybe he was more tired than he knew. Daniel looked at her name tag. She'd printed her name in large, block letters.

Abby Silver. The name went well with the black hair and enormous green eyes.

He glanced at his notes. This was his last seminar for a while. The next eight weeks were to be his first vacation in three years. The first unscheduled time he had allowed himself since his accident three years ago.

Daniel put his pencil down and looked up. "That about wraps up what I have to say. I'll be glad to take your questions now."

The first hand up in the air surprised him. She was the last person he would have expected to have a question.

As surely as the chemistry that had flashed between them earlier, he now received different vibes. The set of her mouth reminded him of the Mona Lisa. Part smile, part resolution. Her shoulders were squared as if she had accepted some private, mental challenge. Lifting the glass on the podium, Daniel took a drink of ice water and wondered at the sudden dryness in his throat. Every instinct warned him Abby Silver was up to something.

"Yes?" The mercury gray dress she wore provided a perfect backdrop for her jet black hair.

Abby Silver stood up, wet her lips, and said, "I own a small craft store in Carbon Canyon. It is in trouble since a big outlet plaza opened a mile away from it. What would you suggest I do?"

She looked the craft-store type.

"As you run a specialty store you might consider advertising in craft and women's magazines. My other recommendation would be to convert the store into a mail-order business and reduce your overheads."

Abby had to fight the urge to sit down. The thought of Gran kept her on her feet. The answers she had received wouldn't help their immediate problems. She had come here for concrete suggestions and she meant to get them.

Raising her voice a pitch, Abby asked, "How much actual experience do you have in helping small businesses?"

The silence in the room confirmed she had actually said the words aloud. Daniel Hawthorn's eyes widened as he said, "Excuse me?"

"I'd like to know if your seminars are based on actual experience, or on theories."

She heard the fat sizzle at the exact moment that it hit the fire. A low hum of conversation went around the room. It was followed by an expectant silence.

"As I said earlier, I have my own import-export business."

Abby ignored the coldness in his voice. If she stopped to think about it she would lose. The rush of adrenaline that had spurred her into challenging him was already draining away.

"I know. This pamphlet..." Abby waved it in the air "...says you have a turnover of a million dollars. That's hardly a *small* business. Solutions to problems for large enterprises may not always apply to a store like mine. Maybe you should leave the word small out of the title of your seminar. That way you won't mislead people in future."

A chorus of agreement came from the rest of the audience.

Daniel looked at the woman and wondered why he had labeled her a failure. She might not know how to operate a small store successfully, but she had a great career as a rabble-rouser. He would never have pegged her as one. Which only went to show he was more in need of a vacation than he'd thought.

"I never attempt to mislead my audience," he said coldly. "If you'll make an appointment to see me in my office, I can discuss your business problems more fully with you."

"I can't afford to make an appointment with you, Mr. Hawthorn," came the quick reply. "This seminar has taken the last of my money."

The surge of adrenaline hadn't lasted long. As it ebbed, Abby knew she shouldn't have challenged Daniel Hawthorn. Humiliation wrapped her like a second skin. The only thing she had achieved was to draw attention to herself.

Daniel stared at her as she sat, her head bowed as if she didn't want to look at him. Irrational guilt chafed him like a hair shirt. He looked around the room. The sea of hands that shot up told him he could ignore the woman and go on to answer other questions. Daniel didn't want to take the easy way out. His personal integrity was at stake here. She had as good as implied he didn't know what he was talking about.

"Let me know if there's any other way I can help you."

Abby raised her head. How could he help her when he didn't know how The Busy Bee was run? If his offer of help was genuine, there was still a slim chance. Desperation forced her into risking everything on one last throw. "The only way you can help is to come to Carbon Canyon, and give me on-the-spot recommendations."

Daniel frowned. She was asking the impossible.

"I'm afraid that's out of the question."

He saw the light in her eyes dim, her shoulders droop. Her expression conveyed she hadn't expected anything more from him. "I thought you might say that, but I had to give it a try."

"Mr. Hawthorn..." He turned away to look at the person who had called out to him.

The rest of the audience was getting impatient and he concentrated on answering their questions. They surrounded him at the end, to shake hands, congratulate him, ask him to autograph his latest book. When the crowd cleared he looked at the seat she had occupied. It's emptiness was like a reproach spoken aloud.

After Jerry Mancini, his personal manager, ushered the last person out, Daniel sank into the chair Abby Silver had occupied. His gaze went to the podium.

Had he really ceased to care about the content of his speeches? It had taken a total stranger to point out flaws he should have been aware of himself. The emptiness that was so much a part of him these days returned in full force.

I should never have come.

Her words haunted him. Daniel rubbed a hand against his temple. According to Jerry, he'd become a phenomenal success. If he was one, why hadn't he been able to help Abby Silver?

He couldn't remember details, only impressions. Eyes as dark as shadows. Vibrant, luxurious hair. The direct gaze, the questions at odds with the trembling lower lip. Abby Silver had managed something no woman had in the last three years. She had gotten under his skin.

This seminar has taken the last of my money.

The ring of truth in her voice as she had stated the fact made him feel like a criminal. His mind refused to let go of his last glimpse of her. Defeated, sad, *without hope.*

His stomach tightened. The feeling was a familiar one. He had been like that three years ago. Today was the anniversary of his accident. Daniel flexed his hands. Their stiffness was a grim reminder that life was like a board game... unexpectedly one could suddenly find oneself back at the starting line. He didn't like thinking he was partly responsible for pushing Abby Silver to that point.

Her suggestion that he make a personal survey of the store was impractical. If he set a precedent like that, others would expect the same from him. He'd had to turn it down.

I didn't think you would, but I had to ask.

Daniel sighed. She'd inferred he wasn't the type to bother about a small cog in the big world of business.

Had success hardened him to the point where he really didn't care about people anymore? He had conducted these seminars for three years. No one had ever challenged him, judged him and found him wanting.

It wasn't a comfortable feeling to know Abby Silver had done all three. That she might be right.

If he couldn't put into practice what he advocated in these seminars, he was no better than a con artist.

"All set for your vacation?" Jerry sank into the seat next to him.

"All set," Daniel said automatically.

"Still don't want to tell me where I can contact you?"

"No."

If Jerry knew where to reach Daniel he would call every day with a different scheme for doubling his money. Only Daniel didn't need any more money. He was taking this vacation to prove something to himself. For the last few months a growing restlessness made him wonder if this was all there was to life.

Fame, success, *emptiness.*

Since his accident, Daniel had let Jerry arrange his life for him. Conducting seminars had led to writing books on business. Overnight success had made him a public figure, very much in demand. For a while he had gone with whatever Jerry had suggested. Now it was time to pull back, to stop and think about the direction his life was taking before it was too late.

The bleakness inside seemed to reach gigantic proportions today. He had everything. He had nothing. Daniel didn't welcome this self-searching. His thoughts forced him to consider what he was going to do about the way he felt. The decision to start the year with a vacation was the right one. He'd be away from the middle of January to the middle of March.

Telling himself he needed nothing more out of life was no use. The reflection Daniel had seen of himself in Abby Silver's eyes confirmed what he had begun to suspect about himself.

Career-wise you might be a wonder, Hawthorn. As a man you're out of touch with the rest of the world.

"That went very well, don't you think?"

Jerry's self-satisfied voice irritated Daniel.

"I guess." If he could blot out the memory of a face etched with worry.

"So, where can I reach you?"

Jerry's casual question didn't fool Daniel. A corner of his mouth lifted as he said, "I'll contact you when I get back to L.A."

Jerry wasn't content. "At least tell me if you're going to be out of the country."

Suddenly the vague plans Daniel had made crystalized into one clear picture. A pair of green eyes framed by a tumble of black hair, looking at him as if he'd given a new name to the word lowlife.

What was the name of that place she had mentioned? Carbon Canyon?

Daniel knew exactly what he was going to do. "Relax, I'm not even going to leave the state."

Calories never helped solve any problems, but the chocolates definitely offered temporary consolation. Food should be included in the top-ten list of dangerous addictions, Abby reflected as she popped a chocolate into her mouth. The glance she gave the box on the passenger seat elicited a groan of dismay. She hadn't meant to eat so many.

It was all *his* fault.

Daniel Hawthorn, with his man-of-the-world air, had upset the balance of her mind.

She'd seen the shock in his eyes when she'd asked him how many small businesses he'd helped. Abby popped another chocolate into her mouth. She wasn't quite sure what had gotten into her. Gran would never believe her granddaughter had stood up in front of a crowd and challenged a man who was obviously an expert in his field. Abby almost didn't believe it herself. She ran a hand through her hair. It had been years since she had acted on impulse.

You've got a brain, Abby. Why don't you use it?

Wishing her late husband's gibes didn't haunt her still, Abby looked at the next sign. She had another ten miles to go.

The sixty-five-mile drive, each way, hadn't been easy. Neither was renting a car to make the trip. All in all it had been a complete waste of money.

This morning she had been sure Daniel Hawthorn would produce a solution to Gran's problems. Far from pulling the rabbit she wanted out of his hat, the man had unsettled her, revived memories of a marriage that hadn't worked. Made her feel stupid.

The bare trees bordering the freeway seemed like the future. Grim. Maybe they should have followed Mr. Hawkins's advice and foreclosed in December. That way, he'd told them, they'd get some money back in taxes and be rid of a white elephant. The decision to wait till the end of January had been a mutual one.

You haven't lost till you admit you've lost, Gran had said, and everyone, Abby included, had agreed with her.

That had been in December, when faith and hope made miracles seem possible. In January, there was only the thought of the unpaid bills, foreclosure and all the people who depended on The Busy Bee.

Abby reached for another chocolate, forcing her mind back to the seminar. There must have been something in it she could use.

Daniel Hawthorn's first words had been, "If your business is in trouble refer to the list in my handout."

She tried to recall the list.

Self-confidence was the first trait on it. Abby's had shriveled in the course of her marriage, and she had no idea what to do about it. Maybe she should have asked the so-positive Mr. Daniel Hawthorn if he gave seminars on self-confidence as well.

Motivation was next. She had plenty of that. The Busy Bee had to stay open, no matter what it took. It wasn't only a retail enterprise. It was a life-support system for people in Gran's age group who gathered there to talk and network.

Decisiveness had been the third word on the list. Abby ran a hand through her hair. Her decision-making abilities were on par with her self-confidence. Nonexistent. Rod had contradicted everything she had said or done till it had become easier to simply leave the decisions to him.

Trying to focus on what came next, Abby drew a blank. Oddly enough she remembered the way Daniel Hawthorn's suit had matched his dark brown hair more clearly than she remembered anything else he'd said. His expression had conveyed sympathy. She must have imagined the concern in his eyes. The *caring*. Big successful business sharks didn't care about floundering guppies.

Abby reached for another chocolate.

* * *

There was a time when he'd thought success and public approval added up to happiness. Lately, Daniel hadn't been so sure. At thirty-four, it was time to discover the reason behind his discontent before it was too late.

Daniel sat in front of the store, staring at the sign above it. The Busy Bee. A strange name for a store. It had taken a while to find. The signs beside the road, advertising the craft store, hadn't been very big. A sweeping glance showed that except for his car, the parking lot was empty. Abby Silver's problems were genuine.

Had he bitten off more than he could chew?

You can always turn around and leave, Hawthorn. You're on vacation, remember?

Today, his first free Saturday in ages, he had wrestled with his decision to stop at Carbon Canyon. As he'd packed his things this morning, he'd realized whichever way he looked at it he knew he had to make this stop. It was the only way he'd be able to enjoy the rest of his vacation.

He had left L.A. at three. It was almost five now. Daniel looked at the painted sign in front of the store. The Busy Bee stayed open till six on Saturdays and Sundays.

Daniel noticed the huge stuffed giraffe staring at him. He wasn't positive he could name all the other items in the window. Some pieces looked like lace, others had flowers and scenes on them. So, this was the merchandise a craft store carried. How large could the market for this kind of stuff be?

Behind the store, a little to the right, was another larger building with a well-tended front lawn. Abby Silver's house?

Turning, he looked at the German shepherd in the seat beside him. Patting the dog's head he said, "I won't be long, Princess. Stay."

The cool evening breeze ensured Princess would be comfortable with the window down. Stopping at a rest area two miles back to give her a drink of water and let her stretch her legs had been a good idea.

As soon as he found Abby Silver he would ask her if he could let Princess out. On the end of a long leash the dog would be quite happy under the enormous tree in the yard. Making a quick assessment of the situation and giving his recommendations shouldn't take more than a couple of hours.

Abby smiled at Mrs. Jacobs as she handed her a bag. "I'm sure your daughter's going to love the lace tablecloth."

The woman nodded, "All Clara's got in her house is an old plastic cover. She's always loved nice things. Losing the baby was very hard on her. I wanted something really pretty to cheer her up. You're sure you don't mind my paying for this with the eggs, Abby? I'll bring in a fresh dozen twice a week."

Abby looked at the careworn face, the anxiety in the faded blue eyes. Gran had started the barter system for people like Mrs. Jacobs.

"That'll be fine," she said gently. "Don't worry about it."

As Mrs. Jacobs left, Abby glanced at her list of things to do. Picking up the box of stuffed toys, she looked around for the best spot to display them.

From the community room, to the right of the shop, came the murmur of voices. Abby could picture the scene in there. Gran with her sewing circle in one corner. Hamish's wood-whittling group busy in another. Mrs. Patel, by the window, bent over her sewing machine, her glasses perched on the edge of her nose. There were others, too, people who came to work or attend the classes or simply to talk.

Carbon Canyon was a very popular retirement community. Opening The Busy Bee had been Gran's way of forming a vital network for people in her age group.

A network that was now in danger. Abby's eyes dimmed. Mr. Hawkins, the manager of the bank, had been most apologetic over the telephone this morning, but he could no longer extend them time or credit.

Of the four weeks they had left, three days had already dripped away like water from a leaking faucet.

The sound of a car pulling up in front of the store brought Abby's head around. She hoped it was another customer.

Daniel ducked his head as he pushed the swing door open. It reminded him of the ones he'd seen in western movies. When the hero went through them, trouble always followed.

"What are you doing here?"

The breathless voice was familiar. He turned his head and saw her behind the cash register.

"Hi!"

He liked the jewel brightness of the green dress Abby Silver wore. Though the loose shape hid her body completely, its color suited her to perfection.

"I was just...er...passing by...and thought...er...I'd stop by and take a look at your store." This couldn't be him stammering.

"Why?" Abby's heart had jumped into her throat at the sound of his voice. There was no real reason for him to be here. No real reason for the fact her legs were so shaky.

"I thought I might be able to give you a few constructive suggestions, if I saw the store...maybe took a quick look at the accounts."

Stunned, Abby kept quiet. She had never imagined this in her wildest dreams. Daniel Hawthorn, business genie, was actually *here* in The Busy Bee.

What was the matter with Abby Silver now? She had her I-know-you-won't-be-able-to-help-us-look in place.

Daniel tried to suppress the guilt he felt.

"Where are you going to spend your vacation?" Obviously Sarah Trenton didn't feel her questions were out of line.

"Yosemite." That had come to him at the spur of the moment.

Sarah Trenton frowned. "Do you have chains for your tires? Surely you don't plan on getting there tonight? It's going to be dark in a couple of hours and those mountain roads are treacherous, with snow on them. Why don't you have dinner and spend the night with us? It will be no bother at all for a friend of Abby's."

Beside him, Daniel heard a gasp of surprise. Before he could turn down Sarah's invitation, he heard Abby Silver say, "Mr. Hawthorn has a very busy schedule. He can't stay." The words were followed by a light touch on his arm. "Let me show you out."

Daniel stared at her. Her eyes held a warning he couldn't understand. *I want you to leave. Now.*

He didn't want to stay, but neither did he want someone else making the decision for him. Irritation crackled through him as he nodded to Sarah Trenton and hurried after her granddaughter.

Chapter Two

"Wait, just a minute."

The hand he placed on her shoulder when they were back in the shop stopped Abby Silver. She spun around to face him, her color bright.

"Why are you rushing me out of here as if the place is on fire?"

"Because I saw the way you looked when I told you Gran was a partner in the store."

"And what way was that?" Did Abby Silver think she could read his mind?

"Horrified."

She *could* read his mind. Horrified described exactly how he felt. Dealing with someone like Abby was different than dealing with her grandmother. He knew that from experience. His father's mother hadn't believed in change.

"I thought *you* owned the shop."

Abby held the door open. "I own a quarter of it."

"I still don't understand why you're rushing me out like this."

She looked at him and then away, but not quickly enough. Daniel saw the anger in her eyes.

"For someone to help The Busy Bee they have to understand and accept Gran and our friends. You said at your seminar that business and emotion are like oil and water. Here at The Busy Bee, they're not. Take away emotion and there would be no need to keep the store open."

She had touched a nerve, hinting he was a stranger to emotion.

"And you think I won't understand that?" Daniel asked.

Her eyes looked at him from head to toe. "No."

"Why not?"

"Your talk that day. You never mentioned the human factor in relationship to business."

Daniel stared at her. He hadn't considered the human factor before. To succeed one had to separate the two.

After a moment she said slowly, "You're a big successful businessman, Mr. Hawthorn. We're not in your league. Our small store isn't run on any hard-and-fast rules laid down by a man who has no idea how we operate. At The Busy Bee we make our own rules as we go along. The old-fashioned way we do things would only upset you."

Except for pushing him out, she was doing her best to get him to leave.

"You think I'm beyond understanding someone like your grandmother?"

Abby Silver took for granted what he had just begun to suspect. That he was out of touch with the complexity of human relationships. What she didn't know was he intended to do something about it.

"I think you've reached a stage in your life where you don't have time to care about people. Not people like us anyway. What's a small store in Carbon Canyon going to do for your image? You're better off helping a firm that will bring you publicity, increase sales of your books, get you more requests to speak.''

Daniel hadn't been so smash-something angry in a long while. That she had drawn such a perfect picture of him didn't help. He turned on his heel and headed back to the community room.

"Where are you going?"

Daniel ignored Abby's cry.

Adrenaline coursed through Abby as she watched Daniel Hawthorn disappear. What was it about the man that made her forget everything and say what was on her mind?

She couldn't go after him, make a scene in the community room. One look at her, and Gran and some of the others would know how upset she was. What did Daniel Hawthorn have to say to them?

Mixed with the flicker of apprehension was a tremor of inexplicable excitement. She'd better get back to arranging the plush toys she'd taken out of the box.

Everyone looked up as he pushed open the door of the community room. For a moment Daniel wanted to turn and run. Maybe this wasn't such a great idea after all. He was no good with people in this age group. If communication became a problem, that would impede progress.

As silence spread across the room, Daniel looked at Sarah Trenton and said, "I'd like to take you up on that invitation to stay for dinner."

He decided to wait until after dinner to offer to look at the books. Maybe food would change Abby Silver's disposition.

Sarah looked at him intently and then said, "We'll eat in half an hour. Why don't you let Abby show you around till then?"

Daniel looked behind him, but she wasn't there.

"I wonder where Abby is?" he heard Sarah Trenton say.

"I'll find her." Daniel turned away quickly.

Don't bite off more than you can chew, Hawthorn. You need time for yourself, remember?

That he did. But Daniel knew he couldn't concentrate on himself till he took care of this matter.

"You're a good dog aren't you?"

Daniel had never heard Abby use that tone of voice before. Gentle, soft, *tender*. She stood by the door of the store, her gaze on the sole occupant of his car.

Stepping to her side at the edge of the verandah he said, "That's Danube Princess. Would you like to meet her?"

Abby hadn't gotten over her surprise at seeing the dog. "I didn't think you'd have a dog."

"You mean I'm not the dog type?" he asked dryly.

That was exactly what she had thought. People kept dogs for companionship. To dispel loneliness. Daniel Hawthorn looked as if he never needed anything or anybody. Embarrassment had bright color flooding Abby's face.

As Daniel stepped forward, the German shepherd stood up on the car seat and gave a whimper of delight. There was no doubting the affection the dog had for its owner.

"Good girl." Daniel said, patting the dog. "Good girl."

The warmth in his voice was real. Abby frowned. He seemed so different from the successful businessman she had seen the first day. Who was the real Daniel Hawthorn?

"Come and meet her."

"Princess," Daniel commanded, as Abby reached his side. "Shake hands with Abby." Looking at Abby he said, "Put your hand out, please."

The dog put a paw into Abby's outstretched palm and Daniel's hands covered both theirs. "Good girl, Princess. Remember, Abby's my friend."

Abby felt her face burn. Daniel's touch was warm, but impersonal. There was no reason for her heart to tick like a time bomb.

"She knows you now, but don't risk trying to approach her when I'm not around."

If Daniel Hawthorn looked at her he would see how flustered she was. Abby bent her head. Her gaze fastened on his hands, narrowing at the sight of the scars there. Surgery scars.

As if he'd realized she was staring at them, Daniel Hawthorn let her hand go, stood up and slipped both his hands into the pockets of his pants.

To Daniel's surprise, Abby brought her hand up and let Princess sniff it, before beginning to tickle her neck. "You're a sweetheart, aren't you?"

Princess sat with her eyes half-closed, her tongue hanging out. It was her happy look.

Daniel stared at the picture. Princess never let anyone else touch her, not even Ed, the assistant he'd had for the last three years.

"She likes you."

Abby's face was hidden behind the curtain of her hair. "Maybe it's because she can smell my dog on me."

"You have a dog?" He hadn't seen signs of one around.

Abby nodded. "Muffy's a wanderer. He's probably in the woods behind the house giving the rabbits a reason to exercise. He'll be back soon. He's not a pedigree dog, but he's clean and well behaved."

Daniel sighed. Now, she was assuming that his dog was like the image she had of him. Cold, polished, uppity.

They both turned as Sarah Trenton hailed them from the house.

"I'm staying for dinner," Daniel said casually.

"Why?" Abby Silver wore her keep-out look again.

"Because I have some time to spare, and I thought I'd look at the books and see if I can offer some constructive suggestions. That way I won't feel I've robbed you of the money you paid for the seminar."

Abby's face flamed. "You don't have to do that," she said stiffly. "We'll manage."

It was a long time since Daniel had come up against so much stiff-necked pride. Usually he had a hard time protecting himself from people who wanted his help.

"I know I don't have to do that," said Daniel Hawthorn. "I *want* to do it."

"I can't pay you," Abby said bluntly.

"I didn't ask for any money," Daniel pointed out coldly. She stared at him, her eyes narrowed, as if trying to analyze his motives. Why was he agreeing to stay and help? Hostile women weren't his style at all.

Abby's head said this was the best thing that could have happened to her. Her heart...Abby let out a tiny sigh...her heart was misbehaving, the way it had since she had first set eyes on Daniel Hawthorn.

Nothing was more important than protecting herself from this avalanche of emotions. Nothing, except helping Gran.

Daniel heard the tiny sigh. It told him he had won this round.

Before they sat down to dinner, Daniel met the other two partners. Hamish McArthur was a retired chef whose hobby was wood carving. His wife, Agnes, loved sewing. Both conducted classes, as well as turning out merchandise for the store. They lived in the house with Sarah and her grand-daughter.

Daniel wondered if the uncomfortable feeling inside was a throwback to the times when he'd been with his grandparents. Meals had always been eaten in silence.

Sarah smiled at him across the table and said, "Do you live in Los Angeles, Mr. Hawthorn?"

"Please call me Daniel," he said. "Yes. I've lived in the Los Angeles area since my college days."

"Abby tells us you're a very important businessman. How long have you two known each other?"

Daniel stared at the dark head, bent over her plate. "A while," he said cautiously.

Sarah sighed. "It's so nice when old friends visit, isn't it, Abby?"

Her head came up. Green eyes looked at him and then away. "Yes."

"If you'd like to use the telephone to call your family, or the motel you have reservations at tonight, please go ahead," Sarah suggested.

"I don't have any family, and I didn't make any reservations," Daniel said evenly.

Sarah smiled as if she'd guessed that already. "Where do you live in Los Angeles?"

"I have a penthouse suite in the Castilian."

"That must be very lonely." Sarah exchanged an eloquent look with Agnes McArthur. "No wonder you're so thin."

The conversation was becoming too personal. It was time to change the subject. "Abby told me you were having problems with the store. I stopped by to see if there was anything I could do to help." Opposite him he saw Abby open her mouth. Daniel said quickly, "As The Busy Bee has four owners, I want to ask all of you if it would be all right for me to take a look at the store accounts. I've already talked it over with Abby and gotten her opinion.''

He looked at her and saw the anger shooting out of Abby's eyes.

"How kind of you." Sarah beamed at him. "We couldn't possibly bother you while you're on your vacation."

"I have no definite plans."

"Maybe it would work out," Sarah said slowly after exchanging a look with her friends. "You look in need of a good rest. You could stay here and we could take care of you while you help us."

"I planned on staying in a motel in town." He didn't need taking care of.

"Helping has to be a two-way street," Sarah said firmly. "If you won't let us take care of you, we can't let you help us."

So now he knew where Abby Silver got her stubbornness from.

"We really shouldn't bother Mr. Hawthorn," Abby interjected. "He needs his vacation."

"I thought you two were friends," said Sarah. "Why do you still call him Mr. Hawthorn?"

Daniel enjoyed the way Abby blushed.

"A slip of the tongue," he said smoothly.

"Spend the night with us," Sarah coaxed.

"Maybe I could stay here tonight," Daniel told Sarah.

"No, you can't."

Everyone looked at Abby in surprise.

"You invited me to come down and give you on-the-spot recommendations, remember?" Daniel couldn't keep the dryness out of his voice.

"I don't want to ruin your vacation." There was more than concern in her eyes. Abby's nervousness amounted to fear.

"You won't," Daniel told her.

She looked angry. For the first time since he'd sat down for the meal, Daniel felt a little better.

"How long a vacation are you on?"

Abby wasn't fooled by the innocent question. Gran could be both deep and wily.

"Eight weeks."

"Ah." Sarah's smile widened. "So spending a little time with us isn't going to hurt."

A few days? Before Daniel Hawthorn knew it, Gran would be arranging the whole eight weeks. Abby wasn't about to let that happen.

"Mr. Haw—I mean, Daniel will be leaving tomorrow as soon as he's looked at the books. Excuse me." Abby began to clear the table.

Abby knew he had to leave as soon as possible. For her sake. It was upsetting being around him. Upsetting to feel like this.

Daniel had no intention of staying a minute longer than was absolutely necessary. Making his suggestions would rid his mind of the burden it had carried around since Abby had challenged him. Once that was done, he had every intention of having the vacation he had promised himself.

"Tomorrow's Sunday," Sarah pointed out. "Surely he's not going to work on Sunday."

"That's for Mr. Hawthorn to decide," Abby said as evenly as possible.

Trust Gran to come up with something like that. It didn't matter that the store was open on Sunday. It was simply a ploy to keep Daniel Hawthorn here as long as possible.

Sarah nodded with assumed meekness. "Will you show Daniel the guest house and the office?"

"I can't," Abby said quickly. "I have to take Muffy to the vet."

The dog that was out in the woods somewhere? She should have come up with a better excuse, Daniel thought wryly.

"I'll be glad to show you around," Sarah said.

Abby wasn't sure how much damage Gran would do in this mood. It was safer not to leave her alone with Daniel. "I just remembered Muffy's appointment is for tomorrow, not tonight," she said. "When you've finished your coffee, I'll take you to the guest house."

Abby decided to keep the tour brief and businesslike. She showed Daniel Hawthorn the office off the store and the community room, then took him around the back and opened the door of the guest house.

"The store was built four years ago when Gran and Gramps came up with the idea of starting it. They added the guest house and the attached carport for their friends who visit."

Daniel sensed Abby didn't like being his guide. It was all there in her tone and the stiff way she held herself. Stepping past her, he entered the guest house and looked around. There was a living room, a bathroom with an adjoining bedroom and a tiny kitchenette. Off the bedroom was a small patio. Beside it was the dog run.

Returning to the living room he said, "It's very nice."

He liked the brown-and-cream color scheme, the vase of red roses on the coffee table. Like the store, the simple elegance of the place appealed to him.

"Thank you. There are towels in the chest of drawers and toilet articles in the bathroom. If you need anything else, call the house. There's a telephone in the bedroom, with numbers beside it."

"Do you know where the second door in the bedroom leads?"

"That goes into the community room," Abby said, "but it's locked. You'll have complete privacy."

Daniel realized she'd sensed he was a loner. Though she lived here with the trio, Daniel felt Abby was a loner, too.

"Breakfast is at seven," Abby added.

"I don't expect to have every meal fixed for me," Daniel protested.

She looked at him and the anger in her eyes surprised him. "Gran expects you to have all your meals with us. She'll be hurt if you don't. While you're here, you'll have to accept her hospitality."

Daniel sighed silently. He didn't seem to have a choice. Protecting her grandmother seemed Abby Silver's first priority.

"I'll see you in the morning."

"I have some errands to run tomorrow, but one of the others will show you around."

Daniel stared at the door after he'd closed it. A hedgehog. That's what she reminded him of. Curled up around her problems. Unwilling to ask for help. Unable to deal with them herself.

Proud, prickly, *frightened.*

Remember you're here for the store, Hawthorn. Keep your mind on business.

That was right. By tomorrow evening, he should be on his way.

The next evening, Daniel looked up from the ledgers when he heard a door bang outside. Sarah hadn't said a word that morning about it being Sunday, when he'd asked to see them. Agnes McArthur had shown him the books. Daniel had wondered if she would ever stop talking and let him look at them, but she had finally left.

His initial dismay that the accounts were all handwritten instead of being kept on computer had vanished with his first look at the figures. The neat entries could have been done by a professional accountant.

The outer door opened. Abby walked in and stopped short. "You're still here?"

It wasn't the friendliest greeting in the world. Daniel merely nodded.

Her gaze fell to the books on the table. "You've been busy. Th . . . thank you for looking at them."

Abby hoped the words would cover up her dismay at the sight of Daniel Hawthorn behind the desk. She had stayed away all day, hoping he would be gone when she returned. She'd told herself he'd take one look at the books and decide the situation was hopeless. He wasn't the kind of man to embroil himself in a no-win situation.

All that would be left for her to do would be to put him out of her thoughts and go back to worrying about the store.

There was only one thing wrong with that scenario. Daniel Hawthorn showed no sign of leaving.

As he looked at her, Abby couldn't resist asking, "Well, what do you think?"

"It's bad, but it's not irreparable. I've seen businesses in worse shape."

"If you'll tell me what we have to do to turn things around . . ." Abby began.

Daniel stood up and put one hand into the pocket of his pants. "It isn't as simple as that. I need to make a more thorough assessment before I can give suggestions."

Did he mean he was going to stay here for more than a day? Abby felt as if she had wandered into a patch of quicksand.

Daniel glanced at her and Abby knew immediately it was exactly what he intended. She hadn't simply wandered into a patch of quicksand. She was neck deep in it and sinking rapidly.

"I've told Sarah I'll stay on for a few days."

Abby closed her eyes. "You can't."

The whisper reached him.

Abby heard the note of surprise in his voice. "I beg your pardon?"

She rubbed her hands up and down her arms to warm herself. "You can't stay on."

"You asked for my help in the first place," Daniel pointed out.

He was right. She was behaving like an absolute fool, just because she couldn't stop reacting the way she did to him.

"There's nothing in this for you." She was desperate enough to repeat her earlier warning.

"I've told you before, I don't want anything from you."

"Why do you want to do this?" Abby wet her lips.

"You accused me of misleading you, remember? For my own sake, I have to prove that I can back up what I say in my seminars."

Her and her big mouth. Abby turned to look out of the window.

Daniel stared at the worried face, the rigid shoulders. The decision to stay wasn't entirely based on the need to prove his integrity. Abby Silver intrigued him as no one ever had before. He wanted to know her better.

"Abby, there you are, dear." Both of them turned as Sarah entered the office. "Daniel, that's quite enough work for one day. Relax, and join us at six for dinner, won't you? If you need anything, don't hesitate to ask Abby or one of us."

Abby sighed. Gran was very pleased about Daniel's decision to stay.

Turning to the door, Sarah, said, "Have you met Muffy, Daniel? He's a delightful dog."

"Not yet," said Daniel.

"Where is Muffy?" Sarah asked her granddaughter. "I haven't seen him around."

"I locked him in the garden shed, so he wouldn't bother Mr. Hawthorn's dog."

Noticing the startled look on Sarah's face, Daniel said, "Why don't you bring your dog over to the run? We could introduce him to Princess now."

"All right." Abby's voice held its usual amount of reluctance.

Doesn't want me around herself or her dog, Daniel thought as he switched off the lights and followed Abby out of the office.

He waited with Princess, wondering what the German shepherd's reaction would be to another dog. At the Castilian, Princess had her own kennel and dog run. Daniel had always thought she was a loner, like himself.

Placing his hand on her collar as he saw Abby approach, Daniel said, "Sit."

Abby held her dog in her arms and knelt in front of Princess. The dogs cautiously sniffed each other.

"Muffy's a friend," Daniel said, patting Princess and Abby's dog at the same time. The latter licked his hand.

"I think I'll set Muffy down."

Once on the ground, Muffy reached up and touched noses with Princess. Running to the edge of the fence he looked over his shoulder and gave a small woof of encouragement. Daniel let Princess go as he felt her tug at his hand.

Watching the dogs run around, Abby remarked, "Well, that was easier than I thought."

"Your dog is very friendly."

Abby felt herself tense. Did Daniel mean as opposed to her? The way she felt around him, she couldn't afford to be friendly. One glance at his profile was enough to set her heart hammering in her chest.

"It's almost dinnertime. If you'll excuse me, I have to go in and wash up."

Daniel went into the guest house to clean up as well. He wondered what he'd gotten himself into. The thought of eating all his meals with the family bothered him. He had to try to make it clear to Sarah that he enjoyed fending for himself.

"Nonsense," Sarah said at dinner when he brought up the subject. "There's no need to feel awkward about eating here, when you're doing so much for us."

"I don't want to impose," Daniel began. "I've looked at the books but it doesn't seem as if I'll be able to give you my recommendations right away. I might have to stay a few more days."

Abby glared at him from across the table, while Sarah beamed and offered, "You're welcome to stay for as long as you want to."

"Carbon Canyon is an excellent spot for a vacation," Agnes added.

"Hamish will enjoy having another mouth to feed." Sarah looked at the silent Hamish who said nothing.

"Mr. Hawthorn probably likes his privacy, Gran," Abby pointed out. "He might be more comfortable eating on his own."

"I'll tell you what we'll do," Sarah said after a minute. "We'll find you the spare coffeepot and you can fix yourself coffee in the guest house."

Daniel sighed silently.

"If you decide to stay longer than Tuesday, you can come in and fix your own breakfast, like we all do. Lunch is generally soup and sandwiches. Dinner is the only meal we really all sit down together for."

Daniel looked at Sarah, amazed. The seriousness in her gaze told him she wanted him to accept her invitation to stay on.

"Let us take care of you for the next couple of days, though. If you decide to stay longer, we can talk about the eating arrangements then." Her innocent smile warned Daniel she was up to something. "It will make us feel better about the time and expertise you're giving us, won't it Abby?"

Abby's face was pale. She looked down at her plate but not before he'd seen the flash of nervousness in her eyes.

"Yes, it will." The dead quality of her voice didn't surprise him.

Sarah turned an expectant gaze on Daniel. Left with no choice, he nodded and said, "Thank you."

Maybe in the days ahead, he thought later as he pulled off his shirt and headed for the bathroom, he'd find out why Abby was so nervous around him.

What happened to that great search for self, Hawthorn?

The thought stopped Daniel short. It had been a while since he'd thought of the purpose of his vacation.

You haven't done anything according to plan since you stepped into the store.

Daniel told himself he could think just as nicely in Carbon Canyon as he could anyplace else.

Maybe he should spend part of his vacation having his head examined. Impulses weren't like him. Abby Silver's challenge had brought him to Carbon Canyon and her reluctance to have him here had goaded him into staying. Bruised ego wasn't enough reason to embroil himself in a situation like this.

No matter what the arguments, no matter that he was spending his vacation so strangely, Daniel realized he felt good about his decision. It had been quite a while since he'd experienced this deep sense of contentment. Under the shower, he did something he hadn't done in ages. He whistled.

Abby stared at the sliver of moon hanging in the sky. Far away she heard an owl call to its mate. The sound was comforting, a part of her childhood memories, of waiting in this room for Gramps to come read to her, for Gran to bring her a glass of warm milk and kiss her good-night.

Childhood with its uncomplicated pattern seemed like a dream. Being a grown-up was entirely different.

Why had Daniel Hawthorn agreed to stay on?

Not that she wasn't glad, Abby told herself quickly. On the business level he was the best thing that had happened to her and Gran. It was just that on the personal level she felt unsettled. She hadn't felt this way in a long time, had vowed she would never *let* herself feel like this again.

Abby got into bed and pulled the red-and-white comforter over her. Since Rod's death three years ago, she had carefully buried her feelings. No, that wasn't right. She had buried her feelings *during* her marriage to Rod, not after. It was the only way she had been able to protect herself.

Abby thought of the way Daniel's dark eyes rested on her, of the inexplicable attraction toward him she couldn't quell. She couldn't run the risk of exploring her feelings. Mistakes cost too much.

Closing her eyes, Abby murmured, "All you have to do is keep out of his way. Daniel Hawthorn will be gone by this time next week, and life will return to normal."

* * *

Downstairs, Sarah and Agnes looked at each other as they heard the door of Abby's room shut.

"What do you think brought Daniel Hawthorn here?" Sarah asked.

Hamish looked up from the paper he was reading. "He said he's been thinking of the store since Abby told him about it."

"I'll bet my grandmother's brooch, it's not only the store that brought him here," said Sarah Trenton thoughtfully. "There's something between him and Abby. She avoids looking at him, and he looks at her more than he wants to."

"I never noticed anything like that," Hamish said, returning to his magazine.

The two women smiled at each other in the way women have done through the centuries. There was work at hand. Woman's work.

Chapter Three

Daniel looked up from the accounts ledger as Abby entered the office. It was Wednesday and he hadn't seen her for the last two days. He knew she'd planned it that way.

"Gran said you had a question about the accounting. She also told me you've decided to stay on." Ice would have been warmer than Abby's tone. "How can I help you?"

Her voice trailed away as their gazes clashed. Daniel watched the color flood her face.

"I just wondered about this entry."

He turned the book toward her, ignoring the minute hesitation before she came forward.

"Let me see." The perfume of wildflowers that clung to her surrounded him. She wore a calf-length denim skirt with a long-sleeved red top. Daniel had seen nuns dressed in less.

He knew she had deliberately avoided him the last two days. That she wanted to have as little to do with him as possible.

Beside him, Abby said, "We advanced Mrs. Olney eight hundred dollars so she could visit her granddaughter in Florida. She has a brand-new great-grandson she wanted to see very badly."

"What did you make the loan against?"

Abby frowned. "Against?"

Daniel sighed. "A loan is usually made against some kind of surety."

"Oh that! Mrs. Olney crochets the most beautiful lace tablecloths. She's going to repay her loan in kind."

"I see." His first impression had been right. This was a more-than-difficult situation. "How old is Mrs. Olney?"

"Seventy-nine. That's why it was important that she go and see her great-grandson right away."

That was also a good reason for not lending her the money. Daniel looked at the pencil in his hand. His next question was about the entry against lace tablecloth. It said nine-dozen eggs. Daniel had a feeling it would be better for his peace of mind not to ask about that.

"What's wrong?" Abby asked.

"I'm wondering how to turn The Busy Bee around given these circumstances."

"If you'd like to leave, we'll understand."

He looked at her profile. Abby's theme song was beginning to wear a bit thin.

"Why?" Daniel released the impatience he'd kept such a strict hold on since Saturday. "Because I make you feel uncomfortable? What is it about me that makes you want to run and hide?"

Her mouth fell open and the color left her face. The passing seconds were measured by the loud thumping of his heart.

"There you are." They both looked at Sarah as she entered the office. "I know you want to keep right on working, so I brought you your lunch."

"You shouldn't have bothered," Daniel muttered, though it wasn't any use objecting. Sarah paid very little attention to his protests.

"Balanced, regular meals are important."

Daniel sighed. Giving in took less time than arguing. Besides, he didn't want Abby accusing him of being rude to her grandmother again.

"Daniel's been cooped up in here the whole morning," Sarah told Abby. "Why don't you take him with you to St. Michael's book sale this afternoon? He needs to get out in the fresh air."

"That isn't the kind of thing Mr. Hawthorn likes to do," Abby said quickly.

She looked at him and then away in that quick way she had.

"What is St. Michael's?" he asked.

"It's a retirement community," Abby said reluctantly. "Some of the senior citizens are helping the library with a book sale today. You'll find it very dull."

Maybe this was his chance to get to know her better.

"What time do we leave?" he asked.

The flash of panic that swamped her was ridiculous. Abby Silver had nothing to fear from him. She tried to make herself believe that it was true.

"At two," she tossed over her shoulder as she left the office.

"I'll let you get on with your lunch." Sarah placed the brown bag on the table. "We still feel it would be better if you come up to the house and have something hot."

"This is fine, thank you," Daniel said quickly.

"Eat it right away," Sarah told him firmly. "A young man needs to keep up his strength."

Daniel admitted he *did* need to keep up his strength. Arguing with Abby Silver took everything he had.

Opening the bag, Daniel discovered there was no fork in the bag for the potato salad. If he went into the community room to look for one and Agnes was in there, she would start talking. It wouldn't be easy to get away. Maybe one of the desk drawers would have a fork or a spoon. He'd seen a plastic knife and a napkin in the top one yesterday. Daniel decided to look. The upper three drawers had nothing but old receipts and papers. The last one stuck. When he finally managed to open it, he realized it was filled with photographs. Picking up the picture that had jammed the drawer, Daniel straightened it.

It was a wedding picture. *Abby's* wedding picture. There was a date on the back. Daniel drew in a big breath, let it out slowly. If she had been married five years ago, where was her husband?

"Gran thought you might like some salt and pepp..."

Abby's voice trailed away as she saw the photograph in his hand.

"I was looking for a fork." Daniel cursed himself. He felt like a trespasser. Abby's expression confirmed that feeling.

Something about the look on Daniel's face told Abby he had found one of the old pictures she hadn't got around to destroying.

She stretched her hand out, and Daniel handed the picture over. Abby looked at it in a daze. The smiling younger version of herself seemed like another person. Someone who believed in dreams and happily-ever-after. Rod looked like the prince she had believed she'd found.

"You're married."

"Was," Abby said, tearing the photograph into tiny pieces. If only she could destroy her memories of the past the same way. "He died in a motorcycle accident three years ago."

"I'm sorry." It explained so much.

"It doesn't matter."

She didn't want Daniel to see the tears. Putting the salt and pepper shakers on the table, Abby left the office. Once around the corner of the office, she leaned against the wall waiting for the pain to ease.

In the beginning, it had all been so romantic. Fresh out of college, she had met Rod at a friend's wedding, been swept off her feet by his smooth talk and charming ways. Her pain and grief when she'd discovered her prince had feet of clay and a larger-than-life ego had eaten at her all these years. How could she have been such a gullible fool?

Abby raised her hands and brushed the tears away. She had learned her lesson. As Gran said, Once bitten, twice shy.

She would never let her heart influence any decisions she made. Hopefully at twenty-eight she was wiser and more sensible than she had been at twenty.

In the house Abby took a caramel custard out of the refrigerator. Picking up a spoon she dug into the English dessert as scenes from the past returned. Rod yelling at her, telling her he had married her for her money, that she was a bore. Rod leaving her alone while he made all those "business" trips.

When her spoon came up empty Abby looked down at the bowl and sighed. Being worried cost her in calories she didn't need.

A glance at her watch showed it was almost time to leave for the library. Rinsing out the bowl, she picked up her purse and headed for the front door. Abby caught a glimpse of herself in the mirror Gran had hung in the entryway. Her face was the only part of her where her weight didn't show. There was too much of the rest in her. She didn't seem to be able to get rid of the thirty extra pounds that had crept up on her during her marriage to Rod.

The sight of Daniel leaning against the old van brought Abby up short. She wasn't concerned about spending the afternoon with him. Once she got to the library, she would be so busy she wouldn't have time to think. What bothered her was the fifteen-minute drive to Carbon Canyon library and back. She didn't like the thought of being in the confined space of the van with Daniel Hawthorn for that long.

"Ready?" she asked.

"Ready," he said. "We could take my car if you want."

Abby looked at the van. Rust spots, old tires and rear doors that didn't close properly. It wasn't in peak condition, but it was handy for transporting things. Besides, riding in it would make Daniel Hawthorn think twice about going anywhere with her in future. She certainly wasn't going to ask Hamish for the loan of his car, just for Daniel Hawthorn!

"We'll take the van. I have books in it for the sale."

The front seat had springs no one ever forgot, once they sat on them. Seeing Daniel wince and quickly shift his position, Abby bit back a smile. It wouldn't hurt him to see how the other half of the world lived.

Music filled the van as she started it. Jazz, Daniel noted with surprise, as Abby turned the volume down.

"Carbon Canyon became a city in its own right two years ago," Abby said as she pulled out of the drive. "My grandfather bought land here in the thirties. There was nothing but farms in this area at that time. Gramps taught school in Los Angeles. After he retired, he and Gran decided to build a house here and settle down. Till I was sixteen, our nearest neighbor lived five miles away. Now it seems that every-where you look, there's a new development coming up.''

Filling Daniel Hawthorn in on the history of Carbon Canyon prevented any awkward silences. It would also ward off any questions about her marriage.

"It's a very beautiful place with an away-from-it-all at-mosphere," he said.

"The valley makes a perfect setting," Abby agreed. "Now people have started building on top of the canyon, for the view. With the new developments springing up, the population of Carbon Canyon is expected to double in two years."

"That should be good for business. I read that hand-made articles are very much in demand now."

Abby glanced at him briefly. Since when had Daniel be-come familiar with crafts, and the market for them?

"Agnes gave me a craft magazine to look through," Daniel explained. "I have to know more about the business to be able to help. Tell me, if you get a bulk order would you be able to fill it?"

"No," said Abby immediately. "We wouldn't be able to supply any demands like that. We stock one-of-a-kind items, made by folks who work at their own pace. There's no way to commercialize what they do."

He'd guessed that. The thought that he might contact big department stores in Los Angeles and ask them to consider ordering merchandise from The Busy Bee faded. As a busi-ness idea, it was a good one. As far as The Busy Bee was concerned, it didn't work.

He looked at Abby's hands on the wheel. Her long ta-pering fingers were like her neck. Slender and beautiful. He remembered the slight roughness of her palms when he had introduced her to Princess. She worked hard at everything she did.

The sound of laughter had woken him at six this morning. Going to his bedroom window, he'd seen Abby with Muffy and Princess in the yard. She'd been throwing balls for the dogs to fetch.

Daniel recalled her expression when she'd seen him with the picture. Bleak, cold, *agonized*.

He should never have opened that damned drawer. She hadn't even heard his apology as she'd walked out of the office.

For a man who until last week had only had room for schedules and negotiations in his thoughts, Daniel now found his mind preoccupied with the enigma that was Abby Silver.

As they pulled into the parking lot of the library, she turned to him. Pointing to an area where folding tables were covered with books, she said, "I'll find you when it's time to leave. I'm going to be working over there."

"Right."

Abby obviously didn't want him tagging along all afternoon. Daniel didn't mind. He'd fill in the time looking at books.

He watched her stop and talk to people on her way to the table. It didn't surprise him she knew just about everybody there.

Walking around the tables, Daniel heard himself being called. "Mr. Hawthorn, how are you?"

"Agnes!" He was glad to see a familiar face. "Have you been here long?"

"Since this morning. Would you like to come and sit with me?"

Daniel nodded, gratefully accepting the invitation. Sitting with Agnes McArthur, though she would talk nonstop, had its advantages. Abby was at the next table.

While Agnes sold books, Daniel watched Abby. There was a man in a wheelchair beside her, who looked very frail.

"That's Jack Williams, the oldest resident of St. Michael's," said Agnes, following his gaze. "He had a stroke earlier this year. Abby's very fond of him."

Daniel could see the way Abby's face softened as she said something to Mr. Williams. Her laugh made something in his chest twist.

"I didn't know Abby is a widow."

He wasn't sure he had said the words aloud, till Agnes said, "Yes."

The answer surprised Daniel. For once, Agnes had sounded like her husband, Hamish. Maybe it was because another customer was at their table. Daniel glanced at Abby. She was discussing a book with someone.

Her husband's death must have been a terrible loss to her. He'd felt like that after Eve's death. Though he hadn't loved Eve, he'd missed her. Blaming himself for her death hadn't made things easier. Daniel had felt burying his feelings was the only way to save himself pain. Now, he wasn't sure. Burying his feelings had resulted in this terrible emptiness that gnawed at him.

Abby turned to Mr. Williams and caught sight of Daniel.

"Hi!" Daniel liked the way her voice sounded when she was flustered. Shy, breathless, excited.

"Hi," he returned.

"Daniel, this is Mr. Williams, a friend of mine. Jack, this is Daniel. I was telling you about him."

Mr. Williams turned to Daniel and held his hand out. "How do you do?"

Daniel shook hands, marveling at how soft the man's hand was.

"I won't be a minute," Abby said. "I have to fetch another box of books from the van."

Daniel was on his feet. "Let me get them." The last load he'd seen her carry had looked very heavy.

The stubbornness was back in her voice. "I can manage."

Daniel wondered how long it had been since Abby Silver had allowed anyone to do anything for her. No one made him as angry as she did. Without another word he walked toward the van.

There was no reason for Daniel to carry the books for her. True, the boxes were heavy, but Abby knew she was perfectly used to lifting heavy items.

"That one," she said pointing to a box.

"How many do you want?"

"All of them, but I can get the rest later."

"I may as well bring them now." Daniel picked up the first box. It was heavier than he'd expected. He frowned as Abby reached for another.

"I said, I'll get them," he said curtly.

Abby looked at him in surprise. "I can—"

"Just let your independence take a back seat for a while, Abby."

She looked around nervously. No one was within earshot. "I don't want anyone to get the wrong impression."

Daniel looked at her. What was she getting at? All he understood was the mounting anger within him.

"People might think..." Her voice trailed away.

He could guess. People might think he was interested in her, because he was carrying boxes for her.

"Older people tend to jump to conclusions...."

Daniel put the box down and looked around. Abby was right. A few people including Agnes were looking at them.

"What might they think, Abby?"

The silky tone he used seemed to increase her apprehension. She backed away from him, came up short against the door of the van.

"Maybe they'll think we like each other. Would that be so bad?" Daniel placed his hands on her arms, felt her shrink. "Maybe they'll think I followed you here from Los Angeles because I'm in love with you." He brought his head closer, watched Abby's pupils dilate. Her gaze fell to his mouth.

His natural impatience brushed away all other thoughts. "I don't care what anyone thinks." He couldn't resist the urge to lean forward and brush her lips with his. "Now, they'll have something real to talk about."

Abby didn't move till she saw Daniel deposit the first box of books by her table, and turn around.

She couldn't face him just yet. Slipping around the side of the van, she walked between the parked cars. Stopping beside a motorhome that hid her completely she leaned against it. A hand went up to her mouth. Her heart was beating at double time. His lips had barely brushed hers, so there wasn't any need to feel as if she were free-falling over a cliff.

Why had Daniel kissed her? The I-don't-know-what-to-do-with-you look in his eyes told Abby her first instinct had been right.

The sooner Daniel Hawthorn left Carbon Canyon the better.

Daniel had never met anyone who disturbed him so deeply.

Thought you knew women, Hawthorn?

He'd thought so. Until now. Until Abby Silver.

Where other women created opportunities to touch and caress, she had a hard time being close to him. Watching her put a hand up to brush a strand of hair off her face, he wondered if there was a man in her life. Had someone taken the place of her late husband? He shouldn't have kissed her like that. He had to apologize, and then remember that he was here purely on business.

Abby Silver was not his type. She was too serious. The kiss had been casual. Her reaction had not. Recalling the way she had blushed, the way her eyes had closed, he knew she took everything seriously. Her work, her family, *loving*.

Abby Silver had home and hearth written all over her. He had to steer clear of her.

Daniel hadn't taken anyone seriously since Eve. His mouth tightened. Since Eve, he had skimmed the surface of relationships, telling himself he wanted nothing more.

Abby wished she knew what was going on in Daniel Hawthorn's mind. His gaze bored into her back and she could sense his impatience. He wasn't an easy man to deal with.

Abby ran a hand through her hair. Rod had called her a country mouse who didn't want to change. He had been right. She was all the things Rod had said she was. Plain, old-fashioned, *boring*.

Daniel had kissed her because she'd annoyed him. Nothing else. A man like him couldn't possibly have any other reason for what he'd done. Turning to the next customer, Abby tried to concentrate on her work.

Agnes introduced Daniel to most of the people who came up to the table as a business expert, and a friend of Abby's. After one lengthy conversation with a customer, Agnes turned to him and said, "Most old people suffer from terrible loneliness. Having someone to talk to makes a big difference in their lives."

Daniel had noticed the way Abby spent every spare moment she had talking to Mr. Williams. He wondered what they had in common. He'd always found it hard to talk to his grandparents. Even now it was hard to say anything besides a greeting to the people he met. Agnes was different. So was Sarah. They didn't seem to notice his awkwardness around them. As for the rest...Daniel felt they guessed how uncomfortable he felt.

In the van on the way back, Daniel turned to Abby. "I'm sorry if I upset you."

"When are you leaving?"

As Gran always said, there was no point in beating around the bush. This afternoon had confirmed Abby's worst fears. Daniel Hawthorn's presence was detrimental to her peace of mind.

"When my work here is done."

"We don't need your help anymore."

Daniel couldn't hide his amazement. "What about the business?"

"We don't need your help anymore," Abby repeated.

"You're so determined to get rid of me that you don't care if the bank forecloses?"

"There's nothing you can do to help us at this stage."

Daniel looked at the tree-lined road whiz by. "This is just because of what happened back at the library, isn't it?"

"I don't want to talk about it."

"Who says we're playing by your rules?" Daniel demanded, his anger returning. "Loosen up a bit, will you? A small kiss isn't an attack on your virtue. What are you so scared of anyway? That I might want more?"

No one, not even Rod, had ever talked to her that way.

"You are in no danger from me," Daniel continued. "I never mix business with pleasure. A beautiful woman deserves as much attention as a business venture. Careful evaluation of her needs, deciding the most effective mode of operation, figuring in advance how to maximize potential, can all be applied as effectively to a date as to a business project.''

Abby stared at the road. Daniel Hawthorn must find teasing her as amusing as kissing her. The man was dangerous, and she wanted him out of her life. Now.

The comparison she'd made the first day had been right. Daniel Hawthorn was a shark, and she was a guppy. Challenging him had been her biggest mistake. She was out of her league, out of her depth, *out of her mind.*

''Now we've got that settled, we can concentrate on the store.''

Abby wondered what it was they had got settled. She had never felt less settled in her entire life.

That night Agnes gave Sarah an account of the book sale, finishing with, ''Things went very well. Very well indeed. Daniel is definitely interested in Abby, and Abby...well, she's determined not to be interested in Daniel Hawthorn, but she is. I think it's a match made in heaven.''

In his favorite chair, Hamish rustled the newspaper impatiently and said, ''Hmphf!''

The tickets arrived Friday morning. Abby ripped opened the letter addressed to her. Surprise held her silent as she read the accompanying note.

''Mrs. Soames, President of Friends of the Library has sent two tickets to a play in the Old Millhouse Theater, for Saturday after next. She says it's to thank Daniel and me for all our help with the book sale.''

Abby looked at Gran in dismay.

Sarah, busy arranging lavender sachets in a box on the counter, glanced at her. ''What's wrong? Can't you go?''

"It's not that." Abby stared at the tickets by the cash register. "If Daniel's leaving tonight, he won't be here for the show on Saturday."

"I wouldn't be too sure of that." Sarah smiled at her granddaughter's expression. "Didn't Daniel tell you? He's going to spend a few more days here."

The cushion Abby was holding slipped from her hands. *He's not.* Her mind screamed the words over the pounding of her heart.

"He wanted to meet Mr. Hawkins, but Bill is away on vacation until Monday, so Daniel's decided to stay a little longer."

"I don't think we should take advantage of his good nature." Abby didn't like the way her voice sounded. Soft, squeaky, excited.

Sarah frowned. "We're not doing that. Agnes and I feel he likes it here. His life in Los Angeles sounds very lonely. He doesn't need a solitary vacation as well. He offered to pay for the use of the guest house, but I wouldn't hear of it. He's doing so much for us."

Abby knew she had to get away. Running into Daniel every now and then wasn't doing anything for her peace of mind.

"Lou asked me to house-sit for her. She's going to spend the weekend with Katy in Monterey. The baby's due any-day now."

Katy was Abby's best friend from high school. She lived in Monterey and Abby often house-sat for Lou, while she visited her daughter. It was a valid excuse.

"Very well, Abby," Sarah said quietly.

Abby felt uneasy under that piercing gaze. Gran had always had a nose for lies. "I'll help with the store both days, but I'll spend the nights at Lou's."

"Daniel said something about having a meeting soon. He's going to tell us what we can do to save the store." Picking up the basket that had held the sachets, Sarah patted her bun. "So you see, he might be here for the play after all."

Abby didn't want to go to a show with Daniel Hawthorn. She didn't even want to tell him about the tickets. Since the book sale she had taken care to avoid him.

"Would you like to go instead of me?" she asked her grandmother. "I have things to do that night."

"That's our bingo night."

Abby sighed. The trio organized bingo every other Saturday at the local high school to benefit St. Michael's.

"I don't know what *you* could possibly have to do that night," Sarah stated firmly. "All you've done on Saturday nights for the last three years is wash your hair and watch a video. It will do you good to get out for a change."

Abby looked at the tickets in her hand in dismay. It would have been wiser not to mention them, to pretend they had never reached her. Now that Gran knew about them she would definitely bring the matter up with Daniel. Abby couldn't lie and say she had misplaced them. Which left her with only one option. To mention them to Daniel before Gran did, and make sure he didn't want to go. She also had to call Lou and ask her if she could spend the weekend with her.

Daniel walked softly out of the community room, careful to close the door into the office very gently. Taking a sip of the coffee he'd gone into the community room for, he wondered about Abby Silver's social life. Surely someone as warm and good-looking as Abby would have a boyfriend. Then again, maybe she hadn't got over her husband's death yet.

She hadn't sounded happy about the fact he'd be staying on, but that was something he'd expected.

Pulling the ledger he was examining toward him, Daniel tried to concentrate on his final summing up.

The headache and chills came on very suddenly. One minute Daniel was deciding he'd finished up for the day, the next he was wondering what was wrong. The dull throbbing at the back of his head had intensified and he felt strange.

Going into the guest house he decided he needed some aspirin. A glance at the bed changed his mind. Taking off his shoes he lay down and drew the covers over his head. He'd look for that aspirin in a minute.

Abby looked up as Gran entered the store. She'd just closed the store and begun totaling their sales for the day. It only took one look at Gran's face to tell her something was wrong.

"What is it?" Gran didn't panic unless something serious happened.

"It's Daniel. Agnes took Daniel's laundry over and he didn't answer, so she looked through his bedroom window to see if he was there at all. He's lying in bed with the covers over his head. She called to him and he wouldn't answer. Princess knows something is wrong. She's scratching on his door as if she wants to get into the guest house."

Abby frowned. It did sound strange. Princess had never scratched on the door of the guest house before.

"Where's the key for the other door?" Gran asked.

"We can't just barge into his room," Abby protested. Neither could they leave him like that.

"I'll take full responsibility." Gran's voice was very firm.

Abby fetched the key from the office. She'd meant to give it to Daniel, but it had slipped her mind.

Gran unlocked the door in the community room. "Daniel?" she called.

He was lying very still. Abby watched Gran tug the covers off and place a hand on Daniel's forehead. "He's burning up. He must have caught the flu bug that's going around."

Daniel opened his eyes and stared at them. His headache was worse and his throat felt as if it was on fire. He looked at the bed, and then at Abby and Sarah. What on earth were they doing here?

"You're sick," Sarah informed him.

"I'm not." The croak that emerged startled him. What had happened to his voice?

"You've got a temperature. About 104 degrees, I'd say."

Abby bit back a smile at Daniel's expression. Gran was an expert at reading temperatures by hand.

"I'm never sick."

"Do you have a headache?"

"Yes."

"Aches and pains all over?"

"Yes."

"You're sick."

Abby smiled. Dr. Davisson had once told Gran she was his only serious competition in Carbon Canyon. She could diagnose and cure as well as he could. Some people preferred her methods.

"Stay in bed," Daniel heard Sarah say. "We have to get you out of those clothes and into pajamas."

Bustling over to the drawer, she took out a pair. "We'll soon have you well. There's nothing to worry about. Agnes makes these special brews that will have your fever down in no time. I'll get some balm and rub your chest and back with it. Hamish will make you some of his special chicken soup and strawberry jelly."

Abby leaned against the wall. Gran firmly believed ill-
nesses had to be treated the old-fashioned way. Staying in
bed, a light diet and plenty of fluids. She had no use for
twenty-four-hour cold medicines and carrying on as usual.

"Do you need help changing?"

Daniel snatched the pajamas from her. "No." He stared
at Abby and when she didn't respond to his unspoken plea
for help, he said, "I don't want anyone coming in here.
You'll all get the flu from me."

"We've had our flu shots," Sarah said firmly. "Besides,
we're not as weak as you young people. Rushing around,
eating fast food, never getting enough sleep..."

Abby slid out of the room quietly. Once Gran got started
on that speech it took a while for her to stop. It was hard not
to grin. Daniel Hawthorn, a speaker-and-businessman-
extraordinaire, was about to receive the best home nursing
available. Whether he would appreciate it was another
matter.

When Daniel awoke Tuesday morning, his first sensation was one of overwhelming relief. He had no fever. His
temperature had stayed down since last night. Sarah had
told him if it did, he could get up for a little while today.

Determined to shower and dress before she got there,
Daniel went into the bathroom. As he shaved, he thought
about the last few days.

Sarah had been serious about taking care of him. Daniel
closed his eyes briefly. The brews had been very strong.
Sarah had actually stood over him and made him drink it.
As for the chest rubs, the chicken soup and the jello...it had
all been enough to cure him in double-quick time.

Daniel's razor paused in midair. He wasn't being entirely
fair. The trio had gone out of their way to take care of him.
Their concern had been genuine. One or the other of them

had sat with him when he wasn't sleeping. When the fever racked him they had applied cool clothes to his head. Abby, they'd told him, had taken over running the store, so they would be free to concentrate on him. She was the only one who hadn't had a flu shot.

"Why are you doing this?" he'd asked Sarah once.

"Because we care about you."

Unlimited caring. It was a strange thing to get accustomed to. He understood Abby's love for her grandmother and the warm affection she shared with the others. But he was a perfect stranger. Why did they care about him?

His relationship with the trio had changed in some subtle way. They had taken him in, watched over him. He felt close to them, in a way he never had with his grandparents.

Later that morning, Daniel glanced at his watch impatiently. He had told Sarah Trenton that the meeting would be at eleven sharp in the community room. It was now eleven-thirty and there was no sign of anyone. Striding toward the store he paused in front of it.

Abby had pinned a huge scene with a fireplace painted on it, to one side of the window. In front of it was a rocking chair. She was working on arranging the folds of an afghan over the arm. Daniel stared at the images she was creating. It was a very good idea for a display.

She wore a teal blue shirt that reached mid-thigh and loose black pants. He remembered her stopping by twice a day to ask him how he felt. The trio hadn't let her in past the door.

She saw him and said, "You're feeling better."

"Yes." He hoped Sarah would believe that.

Daniel thought he glimpsed a smile on Abby's face as she bent and picked up a pillow. It prompted him to say, "I'm not going to drink any more of Agnes's medicine."

Abby couldn't help laughing. The defiant note in Daniel's voice made him sound like a little boy.

"It doesn't taste very good, does it?"

"No." The sight of Abby laughing made Daniel laugh, too. It was obvious she'd had the same brews herself.

"The trio are a formidable nursing crew." Abby chuckled. "It almost makes one afraid to be ill."

"Those inhalations are enough to scare a cold away," added Daniel. "What do they put into the water?"

"Eucalyptus leaves."

The thought of Daniel bent over a bowl of hot water inhaling the vapor, with a heavy towel over his head, was too much. He must have wished he had never heard of Carbon Canyon, or The Busy Bee. Abby laughed till there were tears coming out of her eyes.

"Every time I lifted my head, Sarah would say, 'Just a few more minutes.' I haven't sweated so much even in a sauna." Daniel laughed, too. Now it was over, it did seem funny. "You keep sweating and they keep saying, 'More! More! This will clear up the congestion in no time. You young people are so weak.' The worst part is, I did every single thing they told me to."

"Please stop." Abby held her side. It hurt so much, but she couldn't stop laughing.

It was good to share laughter with Abby. Daniel looked at her mouth, wondering what she would say if he kissed her right now.

Abby knew exactly when humor changed to tension. The way Daniel was looking at her sent a chill up her spine. The last few days she'd told herself she had everything under control. The last minute proved she had nothing under control. With one look, Daniel could melt her self-control.

"When will you be leaving?"

Daniel's smile disappeared. His feelings about the trio may have changed, but Abby's determination hadn't diminished.

"Where's your grandmother?"

Abby looked surprised. "She's at St. Michael's today. It's Tuesday."

Daniel didn't know what was special about Tuesdays and St. Michael's. All he knew was Sarah Trenton's absence was a disruption of his plans.

"I told her we would have a meeting at eleven sharp."

Abby looked up at him. "Gran couldn't have realized today was Tuesday when you told her about the meeting. She's absentminded."

Daniel leaned against the wall and folded his arms across his chest. As long as there was going to be no meeting, he had time to talk. "Why has she gone to St. Michael's?"

"St. Michael's operates a soup kitchen. On Tuesdays, Gran and a group of her friends from St. Michael's volunteer at the kitchen."

And that, Abby's tone indicated, was that. Daniel decided his first impression had been right. It wasn't going to be difficult dealing with Abby Silver. It was going to be impossible.

"What about the meeting?" A trace of impatience showed in his voice.

"I'm sorry about that. Maybe we can have it tomorrow morning instead."

Maybe, thought Daniel, if nothing else cropped up.

"The store has to come first," he said grimly, aware that he was more interested in the way Abby's hair looked than the fact a meeting had just been canceled. "You have to get your priorities straightened out."

Abby paused and looked at him in silence. Picking up some odds and ends, she stepped out of the window. "I told you, you wouldn't be able to handle our affairs." The calm note in her voice surprised him. "If you want to return to L.A. we'll understand."

While he was sick he'd thought about returning to Los Angeles, but he'd reached the same conclusion as before. For his own sake, he had to prove he could practice what he preached. And he wanted to get to know Abby better.

Her continued insistence that he leave destroyed the last of Daniel's patience. "I am *not* having a problem dealing with your affairs, but I could use a little co-operation around here."

"You'll get it," Abby told him. "Tomorrow."

She picked up a wooden rabbit and carried it to the window.

Daniel realized what upset him most was he wasn't in control here. Logic applied to a situation had always won before. Here, it didn't stand a chance.

"This can't go on."

Abby heard him. "You have to realize we see the store as a means to an end, not a profit-making venture. Gran started it so people her age will have a place to gather, talk and support each other."

Daniel stared at Abby. Anger had removed the veil of politeness she normally adopted. Her green eyes blazed like polished malachite in her flushed face.

"Growing old isn't easy," she continued. "Keeping busy helps. Working at St. Michael's bolsters Gran's self-esteem, makes her feel needed. I know none of this helps the business and you find it hard to understand."

Daniel wondered how long he had been giving that impression. Just because he expounded business principles in his seminars didn't mean he didn't possess understanding.

Abby's next words took up where his thoughts left off. "Your talks deal with the black-and-white aspects of business. As I've said before, we deal with the gray area of human emotions that, for us, comes first. The kind of work you do has definite boundaries. Caring for others has none. We'll always put people before business."

Before Daniel could say anything, Abby rushed on. "Think about what I've said, and then decide if you still want to complete the week here. If you don't, we'll understand."

Daniel opened his mouth and closed it again. Turning on his heel he went out of the store. He needed time to sort out his jumbled thoughts. He'd never met anyone as determined to push him out as Abby Silver.

Half an hour later he lay on his back in Carbon Canyon National Park and surveyed the sky. Had he made a mistake in coming here? Was he making an even greater one by staying on? Beside him, Princess and Muffy chased each other in the grass.

Thinking a woman could be evaluated like a business project worked with the women he'd known, not with Abby Silver. He couldn't think of a single thing that would make her look at him in a different light.

Daniel put a stalk of grass in his mouth and chewed it. He couldn't leave Carbon Canyon now. She may not want him, but she wanted the store to do well for the trio's sake. He'd seen the look on her face whenever Sarah discussed the foreclosure. Fierce, anxious, *yearning*. More than anything Abby wanted to make everything right for her grandmother. He had to respect that love. He had to help Abby.

The gray area of human emotions has no boundaries.

Red tape, business rivalry, ignorance of business methods—he'd dealt with all these. What he hadn't dealt with was a business that was so closely linked with emotional concerns that he didn't know where one began and the other left off.

This is a good point to pack and leave, Hawthorn.

He had protected himself in the past, let nothing touch his business reputation. If he went ahead with helping Abby, he was going to risk that reputation. Right now his chances of success were small. If he left, he could return to his penthouse at the Castilian. To the old way of life. Safe, sensible...

Empty?

Even before his inner voice supplied the last word, Daniel knew he wouldn't do that. He couldn't quit now.

Tomorrow he would lay his cards on the table, make their options clear to Abby and the trio. That was why he was here in the first place. It wasn't his responsibility to see they implemented his suggestions. That was up to them. All he had to do was make his recommendations and leave.

Daniel realized his original problem of finding out what was wrong with The Busy Bee was now compounded by his own feelings. Abby was an increasingly large part of his determination to stay on.

Deliberately Daniel began to catalog his life. He had made, and was making, as much money as one man needed in a lifetime. He had friends... of a kind. He had a penthouse suite, a dog and a wonderful career. What more could anyone want?

Someone to call your own, maybe?

Daniel shook his head. Rolling on his stomach, he buried his head in his hands. The fact he didn't have an ongoing relationship with a woman was his choice. Since Eve, he had indulged in a few casual relationships. Women whose faces he couldn't even remember. For a long while now there had been no one. Daniel had told himself it was because he had been too busy. The truth was he hadn't met anyone who appealed to him.

A picture of Abby flashed in his mind. Talking to Mr. Williams in a gentle voice. Abby, telling him she would understand if he left Carbon Canyon. Abby, with her hair as dark as night and eyes filled with secret pain. She unsettled him, tied him in knots.

A part of him wanted to solve the mystery behind her pain. Caution, developed over the years, warned him not to stir up a hornet's nest.

Each facet he discovered about Abby was a delicate, fragile link in a chain. Patient, caring, generous, loving. The list went on and on. He had more than he could name. The only link that didn't fit was her nervousness around him.

Daniel knew he wasn't going to cut and run. He couldn't. There was nothing to run *to*. The nagging emptiness inside that had prompted him to take this holiday was still there. He had to come to terms with it before he went back to Los Angeles and his work.

Abby glanced at the sandwich on one of Gran's blue-and-white plates. Only crumbs of the two enormous peanut butter and jelly sandwiches she had eaten remained.

It was all Daniel Hawthorn's fault. He had walked into the store this morning, and her heart had done its usual flip-flop at the sight of him. She had flown off the handle, something she hadn't done in years. It wasn't only because of what he'd said about Gran and her friends. Abby had been furious about the way he made her feel. The man had no right to barge into her life and disrupt it. She didn't need him, or his melt-your-brain-with-one-look gaze.

It was becoming harder than ever to constantly remind herself that feelings couldn't be trusted.

Chapter Four

The next morning, Daniel looked at the trio assembled in the community room. Sarah's apologies and explanations had been profuse. His gaze met Abby's as she came into the room. Daniel felt his stomach tighten.

"Sorry, I'm late." The blue-and-black top she wore over a black skirt made her eyes look greener than ever. "A customer had a question about something we sold her."

Daniel nodded. He knew who would win if it was a toss-up between punctuality and a customer.

"Abby will take notes," announced Sarah. "Shall we begin?"

Daniel looked around the room. There were nine people in here. He recognized Franz Koch who had brought him a card when he was ill, and Lou Wong who had sat with him one evening.

Asking everyone but the partners to leave the room would be unthinkable. The Busy Bee was really community property.

"I looked at your accounts and had a talk with Mr. Hawkins, the bank manager," Daniel began. "The store hasn't made the last three mortgage payments. Because he knows you so well, Mr. Hawkins pulled strings to give you one month's extension. So far the books don't show enough to make this month's payment. We have a serious problem."

An hour later Daniel realized the problem was more serious than he thought. Getting The Busy Bee back on its feet would take more than knowledge and expertise . . . it would take help from the patron saint of all such businesses.

The trio adamantly refused to raise their prices, or change their mode of extending credit to anyone who asked for it. They didn't want to consider closing the store and opening a mail-order business. They looked at the proposed budget he had drawn up, but he knew it would only be followed till they found someone in need.

Rising exasperation told Daniel his initial doubts were right. The trio's attitude brought back memories of the time he had suggested his grandparents move to Arizona because they both suffered from severe arthritis. They had refused, saying they hated change of any kind. So, apparently, did the owners of The Busy Bee.

Abby's load of guilt increased as the morning wore on. It was one thing to cling to their beliefs, it was quite another to expect Daniel Hawthorn to see their point of view.

She shouldn't have challenged him like she had. The trio were like water, Daniel like oil. The two would never mix. The more insistent he got, the more stubborn they became. She could sense his mounting frustration and the tight rein he kept on his temper.

"I'm sorry you find us so uncooperative, Mr. Hawthorn, but you see at our age, profit is not our only concern," Sarah stated firmly. "Having something to do and helping others our age in the process is more important than money."

There were nods and murmurs of agreement from everyone in the room.

Pack and leave, Hawthorn. Forget you ever heard of this place.

Daniel frowned at his notes. He wasn't a quitter. He hadn't come down here merely to offer suggestions. His integrity was at stake here. Running away would prove his ideas didn't work in practice.

He looked around the room. No one had told him it would be easy. "As you don't find my first suggestions practical, we'll have to consider other ways of promoting business. I suggest you have some flyers made and distributed directly to homeowners in the area."

Abby couldn't believe what she was hearing. In spite of their lack of cooperation, Daniel Hawthorn was still determined to help them?

"We can get the flyers printed and distributed," Hamish agreed.

"My next suggestion is going to cost money, but I think the payoff will be worth it. There's a billboard, visible from the freeway, three miles before the Carbon Canyon exit. An ad up there would bring in a great many more customers."

"We'll find a way to pay for it," Sarah said.

"There's just one more thing…" He wasn't sure how they were going to take what he said next. Glancing up to find Abby looking at him, Daniel had no doubt what her reaction would be.

"Yes?"

Daniel looked at Sarah. Her head was tilted to one side and her smile was encouraging.

"There is no way the store is going to be able to make up its arrears in payment by the end of this month, therefore..." Daniel paused. He had to find just the right words to explain.

"Therefore?" prompted Hamish.

Taking a deep breath, Daniel looked at Abby. "I've made the payments on behalf of The Busy Bee." He saw the snap of anger in her eyes and said quickly, "Before any of you say anything, let me finish. It was not an act of charity. You now owe me four months' payment with interest. It's what you owed the bank, with one difference. We have a little more time to come up with a solution for the problems you face here."

"We will pay you back with interest." Abby's fierce comment made heads turn in her direction.

"I expect you to," Daniel said evenly. "I did this so I would have more time to help you."

Fear was a lump in Abby's throat. She ought to be glad Daniel had helped them out. She wasn't. This put them in his debt and she hated the idea.

"I think that about concludes our meeting." Daniel looked around the room.

There was a murmur of thanks before people left. Daniel took a slow, deep breath. The fact he needed time to sort out The Busy Bee's financial problems wasn't the only reason he'd made the payments. He needed time to figure out Abby.

Daniel glanced at the chair she had occupied. He had hoped she'd be a little relieved, but all he'd done was upset her. As usual.

Abby felt the situation was getting worse, not better. Taking a giant bag of potato chips out of the pantry she decided to take it up to her room.

Owing Daniel money made everything worse. Not knowing when they would be able to pay him back increased Abby's worry. Things looked bleak for the store. Yesterday they'd had one customer all morning. Theodore Lucas had picked out a teddy bear for his grand nephew and offered to work in the yard for two weeks as payment.

Everything was so complicated. The people who depended on the store, the money the store owed, Daniel Hawthorn.

Crumpling the empty bag, Abby threw it in her trash can. Gran always said every cloud had a silver lining. As far as Abby could see the horizon was covered with storm clouds, but not a single one had a silver lining.

Saturday morning, Daniel woke and linked his hands under his head. He was getting used to being woken by the sound of birds fighting over the crumbs Abby put out each morning. He could hear friendly growls as Princess and Muffy chased each other in the yard. Princess had changed completely. Gone was the staid, dignified dog he had owned. With Muffy for a teacher, Princess was rapidly making up for all the lonely years she'd spent.

He had completely recovered from the flu. For a few days he'd felt a bit weak, but now he was back to normal.

Daniel realized he didn't have much to show for his first two weeks in Carbon Canyon. The flyers had been distributed yesterday. Hopefully they would bring in some fresh customers.

Abby. The last time he'd seen her had been at the meeting on Wednesday. She was making a career out of avoiding him. Daniel knew she was still mad at him. He'd walked into the store Thursday, but she had immediately started a lengthy conversation with one of the customers about a knitting pattern, and he'd finally left. Pretending he had a question about an entry, he had asked for her Friday afternoon, and been told she was at St. Michael's. She hadn't been in for the evening meal both nights. Sarah had mentioned she was dining with friends.

Daniel knew he had to find a way of making contact with Abby. She couldn't go on avoiding him like this.

Abby looked at the flask of coffee and sighed. Gran's note said the trio were cleaning out the store, and would Abby please take Daniel's coffee over to him?

There had been some talk of finding a spare coffee pot for Daniel so he could fix his own coffee. Obviously it hadn't been found yet. Abby grabbed the flask and strode in the direction of the guest house. It was barely seven. Maybe she could knock on the door, leave the flask on the doorstep and run for dear life. She had to find a minute today to unearth the coffee pot she had used in college. Daniel Hawthorn could make his own coffee in future.

"Hi!"

Abby's head shot up at the sight of Daniel leaning casually against the front door of the guest house wearing burgundy-gray-and-white-striped pajamas, dark stubble, tousled hair and a twinkle in his eye. Above the wild thumping of her heart, Abby heard the sounds of birds in the tree, a tiny bark from Muffy somewhere in the distance. The scent of roses drifted to Abby as awareness etched the scene into her memory. The flask suddenly felt extremely heavy.

"Your coffee." Abby's hand was as stiff as a drum major's as she held the flask out.

"Thank you. Would you like to come in and share a cup with me?"

Abby raised her gaze and it tangled in the matt of hair on Daniel's chest. He hadn't bothered to button his pajama top. "No," she said quickly, looking away. "I have to take Muffy to the vet."

"I see." The dog's trips to the vet were becoming legendary. "I hope there's nothing seriously wrong with him."

"Of course not." Abby looked at him, realized what she'd said and went bright red. "What I mean is he has to have some tests, but he doesn't have anything infectious."

"I'm glad," said Daniel mock seriously.

Abby stood drawing patterns in the sand with the toe of her sneaker. Daniel observed the sunshine glinting off her hair. He liked the plaid scarf draped around her neck, the tiny matching hat perched on the back of her head. He didn't want to bring up the subject of the money he'd paid the bank. It would destroy this tenuous peace between them.

"I have some good news," she announced, looking up at him.

"Yes?"

"Agnes's son by her first marriage is a cardiologist in L.A. He's offered to pay for the billboard."

"He has?" asked Daniel in surprise. "Agnes told me she couldn't get on with her daughter-in-law."

"She can't. That's why we're getting the billboard. Agnes called and told her son she and Hamish would have to move back with him for a while, if the store closed. She says he offered to pay for the billboard right away."

"Clever," Daniel approved.

They smiled at each other, the first real smile they had exchanged in a while.

"Gran says at their age it's the results that count, not the methods."

Daniel nodded. "Who decided what goes on the billboard?"

"I did. I asked for a window in the background with a set of lace curtains. In front of it is a rocking chair with an afghan draped over one arm, a needlepoint cushion and a teddy bear. The caption's going to read, The Things that

Turn a House into a Home. At the side we're going to have the name of the store and directions.''

The scene Abby described was the one Daniel had seen her set up in the window of the store.

''I wanted to give people a sense of coming home, of warmth. That's what we're all about.'' Abby sounded hesitant, as if she wasn't sure she'd done the right thing.

''Your ad sounds intriguing and that's exactly the effect to achieve. Make people want to stop here. I like it very much.''

Daniel watched the color creep into her face.

Coming home. Daniel wondered what it would feel like to come home to Abby.

His gaze dropped to her mouth and he heard her say quickly, ''I called the owner of the billboard. Sam Brite lives in Carbon Canyon and knows Gran. He said business is slow, so he'll see to it right away. We should have the ad in place by Tuesday.''

And he could leave whenever he wanted to. She didn't say the words but they hung in the air between them. The smile left his face. He wasn't ready to leave. Yet.

''What time are we leaving for the play today?'' It was the only thing he could think of, to get her to spend some time with him.

Abby's head shot up and her face went bright red. ''The play?''

Daniel watched her, enjoying the effect his question had on Abby's composure. ''You—you wouldn't like it. I-It's an amateur group and—and...''

Her voice sounded strange. Hoarse, scratchy, *desperate.*

''I think we should give ourselves a chance to find out whether we like it or not. Some amateur groups are pretty good,'' Daniel said smoothly. ''Besides, I've heard the old converted mill is a very interesting place. What time shall we leave?"

Abby scuffed the path with her shoe. Why hadn't Gran kept quiet about the tickets? The temptation to lie and say she had lost them tugged at her.

"Abby?"

Looking up, Abby knew she had lost. She had never been a good liar.

"Seven," she said slowly. "The play starts at seven-thirty."

Daniel watched her hasty retreat.

Now that was smart thinking, Hawthorn.

The tiny amount of guilt he felt was quickly smothered. He agreed with Sarah. Sometimes only the results mattered.

"Never thought Abby would change her mind about going out with Daniel," Agnes stated after dinner that night.

"I didn't, either," Sarah agreed. "I'm glad she told him about the tickets."

Hamish looked up from his crossword puzzle and said, "Leave them alone. It never pays to interfere in someone else's life."

Sarah and Agnes smiled at each other, as Hamish went back to his paper. What did men know? If women didn't give matters a little nudge now and then, the world would come to a standstill.

Abby walked over to the guest house wishing she had never agreed to go out with Daniel Hawthorn. Her legs felt like clay and the rest of her quivered like the bowl of ice cream she had devoured before getting dressed.

She tapped lightly on the door. Maybe he had forgotten all about the play and fallen asleep. Maybe he had changed his mind about the evening. Maybe...

The door swung open and Abby's gaze riveted on the dark hair on Daniel's chest. Why hadn't he buttoned his shirt? Raising her gaze to his, Abby felt a quiver shoot through her. There was a storm brewing in his eyes.

"Abby, come in."

She walked into the guest house, overpowered by the clean soap smell of him. His hair was still shower damp. The dark patches on his shirt testified to an impatient toweling of his body.

"You'll have to help me with my buttons."

The brusque request startled her. Abby raised her gaze to his as Daniel Hawthorn approached and extended an immaculate cuff. "I was in an accident a few years ago. My fingers can't cope with objects this small yet. Normally I use studs in my shirt, but this seems to be the last clean shirt left in my closet, and it has buttons."

Abby stared at him, reminded of the gold cufflinks she had glimpsed at the seminar.

"What kind of an accident?" she asked, remembering the scars on his hand.

Daniel Hawthorn's face became expressionless. "A car accident. Nerves in my hands were damaged, and I couldn't use them for a while."

"I'm sorry." Sorry she had asked. Sorry his hands were damaged.

The blanched look on her face, the softness in her voice made Daniel forget his usual reluctance to talk about the accident.

"I still get very impatient and frustrated when I can't do small tasks like buttoning my own shirt." Daniel couldn't explain the strange need to reassure Abby that his impatience wasn't directed at her. "In the beginning I couldn't use my computer, even sign my name to a document. I told myself it was a case of mind over matter and tried to force myself back to my normal routine. My hands got worse and my neurologist warned me I was doing myself more harm than good by refusing to accept my limitations. That's when I started conducting these seminars."

Abby stared at him. She could imagine how hard it must be for someone like Daniel not to be in complete control of his life. Those who rode with the punches life handed them escaped lightly. Others, like Daniel, resisted them and fared worse.

"It's hard to tell there's anything wrong with your hands."

"Abby?" His extended arm reminded her he was still waiting for help with his buttons.

Abby raised shaking fingers to perform the task for him. The buttons on his cuffs were easy, but the ones on the shirt front were tiny and stiff. As Abby worked her way upward, Daniel's breath stirred her hair. Abby's shaking fingers brushed against skin and the soft cushion of hair on his chest as she went on to the next button. The contact almost made her stop breathing. "I'm sorry."

Her words seemed unnaturally loud in the room. Would he think she was deliberately teasing him? Abby felt Daniel stiffen. She bit down hard on her bottom lip. A fresh burst of nervousness made her fingers feel ten times as large and awkward than they normally were. A quick glance from under her lashes revealed a poker profile. It took twice as long to do the last two buttons.

Daniel watched the stole slip from her shoulders and slide to the floor. Her raised hands made her breasts thrust against the lacy high-necked blouse she wore. With her silky skirt and boots, every bit of her was covered from head to toe. He got the faint whiff of her scent, saw the way she bit her lower lip in concentration as she buttoned his shirt.

Abby acted as if she were a novice breaking every rule in the convent by helping him with his shirt.

"Thank you." Daniel left the room and returned holding his tie and his jacket.

Abby noticed his shirt had been neatly tucked into his pants. As she watched him knot his tie, their gazes linked in the mirror. Breathing became an effort.

Daniel turned to her. Abby looked away quickly. Intuition warned her she had entered a danger zone.

Abby swallowed. The emotion inside her was pure, twenty-four-carat excitement. Heady, sizzling, *strong*.

"Abby?"

The sound of her name broke the spell.

"We don't want to be late," she said, picking up her stole from the floor. "I'll wait for you by your car."

Abby walked out quickly, almost afraid Daniel would stop her, and notice she was shaking like a leaf in the wind.

All through the evening Daniel kept his manner casual. Gradually he sensed Abby relax beside him and let out a silent breath of relief. He didn't want to lose the little ground he had gained earlier. For a few moments he'd felt Abby's barriers were down.

"Would you mind very much if we didn't go home right away, Abby?" he asked as they came out of the old millhouse. "There's something I want to show you."

Abby's heart began to race. That line was one she was familiar with. A prelude to trouble.

Daniel seemed to take her silence for consent. "It's five minutes from here, and you won't have to get out of the car."

Abby forced herself to take a big, slow breath. "All right."

Daniel started driving to the top of Carbon Canyon. Abby's pounding heart confirmed her worst fears. The road led to a spot known as Lover's Leap. She should never have come. Daniel whizzed past it and fear became pure terror. There was nothing beyond except private homes.

Daniel turned off on a dirt road between two houses. Where the road came to an end, he stopped the car and turned to her.

"Look," Abby heard him say.

The lights of Carbon Canyon stretched out below them. Abby barely noticed the view. Her gaze fixed on Daniel, she reached for the door handle.

He had discovered this spot a few nights ago. Daniel liked driving up here at night, sitting and thinking. He lowered his window, welcoming the night breeze that ruffled his hair. Something about the quality of Abby's silence made him turn toward her.

"What's wrong?"

"Nothing."

Her tone made him switch on the interior light. Her fixed expression reminded him of a frightened rabbit. Daniel frowned. Abby wasn't merely nervous. She was terrified.

"What's wrong?" he repeated.

Abby simply shook her head. He put a hand out to reassure her and she shrank against the passenger door.

Daniel's brow cleared. He should have known what was bothering Abby.

"Do you want to talk about it?"

"T-talk about what?" asked Abby, forcing the words through her stiff lips.

"The fact you're sitting next to me acting as if I'm a vampire and you're my next victim."

Abby took a deep breath and found herself choking on the confusion welling within her. "I—I'm not. It's just that this place makes me nervous. "C…couples come up here."

So that was what was worrying her. "Would it help if I told you, I have no intention of grabbing you? I brought you up here because I thought you would enjoy the view. Since I've discovered the spot, I come up here almost every night. It helps me relax."

Abby let go of the door handle, wishing she could vanish into thin air. "I—I see."

"What happened to you, Abby?"

She turned toward Daniel. "I—I don't know what you mean. Can we please go back now? I'm tired."

Daniel had always gone after what he wanted in life. Standing back now, giving in to Abby, was a first with him. Impatience gripped him. Knowing Abby was like a game of snakes and ladders. Every time he thought he'd made a little progress he slid back a whole lot.

"Is it the memory of your husband? Do you feel no one will ever take his place in your life?"

Abby stared at him. "My marriage was a failure before Rod died."

The minute the words were out she covered her mouth with her hand. Now why had she gone and blurted that out? It was the effect Daniel had on her.

My marriage was a failure. That cleared up so much. Abby's lack of confidence. Her nervousness around him. The insistence he should leave.

Putting a hand out, Daniel turned the key in the ignition. "You're quite safe with me, Abby. I've never forced myself on anybody and I don't intend to start now."

"I—I don't know what you mean."

"You do," said Daniel firmly. "The fear and unwillingness you exude is like a red light."

"A red l-light?"

"Yes," Daniel retorted firmly. "Even if I wanted to kiss you, the touch-me-not signals you put out would prevent me from doing so. I have never kissed a woman against her will and I don't intend to start now."

"Signals?" What on earth was he talking about?

"There are stages in establishing a relationship, just as there are stages in establishing a business. First a man and woman are aware of each other. Next they exchange subtle signals that they want to touch, hold, be more to each other. No stage evolves into another without these signals."

Where had he got his degree in the psychology of courtship?

As Daniel set the car in motion, Abby thought of what he had said. *Most men don't proceed till they get a green signal from a woman.* Abby hoped all the signals she put out were red. Bright red. She couldn't afford sending out any other kind.

Abby had the door open as soon as the car stopped. "Thank you," she said, and fled into the house.

Daniel went through his pockets for the key to the guest house. His spurt of impatience had faded. He might have been angry under normal circumstances, but these weren't normal. The fear on Abby's face had been very real. Her marriage seemed to have bulldozed her faith in men.

Daniel put a hand up to his head just to make sure he really hadn't sprouted the horns Abby Silver saw whenever she looked at him.

Abby stared out her bedroom window. She was too keyed up to sleep. Daniel's words relentlessly repeated themselves in her head. The hoots of the owls, calling to each other, failed to comfort her.

Tonight she couldn't take refuge in the soothing influence of old familiar things. The new sensations flooding her mind and body drowned everything else.

Chapter Five

"Where's everybody?" Daniel asked, entering the community room Monday morning.

Hamish looked up from the piece of wood he was whittling in a corner. "Out."

The man would win a prize for Monosyllable King of the Year, thought Daniel.

"Abby said she would be in the store today." He had to see her. Since Saturday night she'd made sure they were never alone.

"She's gone to visit a sick friend."

"Sarah and the others are at a swap meet clear across town," Hamish added.

As usual, business came last.

"Would anyone mind if I opened the store?" Daniel asked.

"Nope," Hamish said without lifting his head.

Daniel went into the store, unlocked the front door and turned the Closed sign to Open. His impatience, he had to admit, wasn't only due to the fact the store hadn't been opened. It was because Abby wasn't around. The word elusive could have been created just for her.

He moved around the store restlessly, fingering the finely crocheted lace tablecloths, the hand-knitted sweaters, the silk jackets. He was thinking more of Abby than he was of the store these days. It was the first time in his life a person had overshadowed his work. He had to make sure Abby didn't sense that. If she guessed what was going on in his mind, she'd have him out of here before he could say a word. To justify being here, he'd have to come up with some more suggestions soon.

Daniel's forehead wrinkled in concentration as he tried to think of a way of improving business. The merchandise was quality stuff. There had to be a way to move it quicker.

"What are you doing here?" Abby's flustered voice from the doorway made him turn around. She was wearing a gray dress with long sleeves that buttoned to her neck. On her the color was stunning. Daniel looked at the tiny black buttons and wished he could reach out and unbutton the top five. Just enough to give him a glimpse of Abby's beautiful neck.

"Minding the store," he said more sharply than he intended.

"Oh! Had many customers?"

"Not one."

"Mondays are generally slow. There's a giant swap meet in Carbon Canyon on Mondays. It lures most of our customers. Agnes and Gran usually buy the fabric and sewing supplies they need there. It's cheaper in bulk."

It also ensured they had plenty on hand to give away, Daniel knew.

Abby turned to leave.

"Where are you going?" Daniel asked quickly.

"To the house."

Hamish entered the store and announced, "The chicken casseroles are ready. Should tide Fred Harper for a while."

"Thanks, Hamish," Abby said. "I'm going back right away. I won't be back for dinner."

"Take care," Hamish called after her.

Turning away, he looked surprised to see Daniel behind him.

"Is something going on at Fred Harper's that I should know about?"

Hamish picked up a piece of sandpaper and began to work on the bird he'd carved. "Fred Harper is ninety-two and blind. His daughter has turned part of her house into an apartment for him. Once a month, Abby goes out to help Nan Harper clean the apartment and stock up Fred's freezer."

He should have guessed it would be something like this.

In the world Daniel came from people hated giving anything, even advice, away free. Abby's problem was that she couldn't stop giving. At this rate, Daniel knew, a year could go by and he wouldn't see much of her. He would have to come up with a better way of spending some time with her. Watching Hamish smooth the bird's neck gave him an idea.

"May I join your wood-whittling class?"

He'd heard Abby discuss the dog she was carving with Hamish and knew she was part of the class.

"Ever whittle before?"

Daniel shook his head, "Only experience of whittling I have is sharpening a pencil with the kitchen knife."

"Why do you want to join?"

This is one man you can't fool, Hawthorn.

"I've had a problem with my hands since a car accident," he explained. "I thought the whittling might improve the dexterity in my fingers."

"Might," came the grudging admission. "You can come to the class tonight."

"I'll be there," Daniel said.

Abby looked around the room. Why on earth had Daniel decided to join Hamish's class? No one else seemed to notice what a hard time Daniel was having with his knife. He wasn't even holding it right. Abby winced as it slipped out of his hand and fell on the floor. It wasn't like Hamish to ignore a new student.

"Sorry," Daniel said to no one in particular as he picked it up.

The knife fell twice more before Abby stood up and went over to him. Enough was enough.

He sensed her approach and looked up. She had changed her clothes. The silky moss-green shirt she wore with brown pants drew attention to her eyes. As their gazes met, Abby looked away. Daniel felt a tightening low in his stomach.

He stopped as he'd done every few minutes to flex his fingers and ease the cramping there.

"Do they hurt?"

For the first time since his accident he wasn't defensive about the state of his hands. "Yes."

Abby's eyes were warm with concern. "Maybe it's the way you're holding the knife. Try holding it the other way as if you're sharpening a pencil. Lay the blade flat against the wood and then move it slowly."

Daniel tried to do as Abby said but the knife bounced right out of his hand again.

"Let me help you."

Abby came up behind him as he picked it up. Standing a little behind his right shoulder she placed her hand over his. "Position the blade almost parallel to the wood. Hold the block with your other hand. Now, move the knife like this."

Daniel was barely aware of Abby's instructions. Her breath was warm on his cheek and her closeness made it hard to concentrate. Turning his head, he looked up at her.

Something in Daniel's expression made Abby drop her hand and turn away quickly. "I think you've got the hang of it now. I have to get back to my own work."

For a few moments Daniel knew Abby had dropped all the barricades she normally put up around herself. His mouth tightened. Had she been motivated by pity? He'd seen how much compassion Abby possessed, but he didn't want any of it.

"Are you imagining the object you want to carve, Mr. Hawthorn?" Hamish's dry voice startled Daniel.

"Yes," he said quickly, moving his knife back and forth at random.

"Good."

Hamish turned away, and Daniel looked at the wood in his hands. If he could, he'd carve a bird escaping from a net, soaring toward freedom.

He already had a name for the bird. Abby.

Abby looked at the bottle of oil. She couldn't put off giving it to Daniel any longer. His hands had been really stiff tonight. The oil would make a difference. Picking it up from her dresser, Abby left the house before she could change her mind. Daniel answered the knock on the door, wearing his jogging shorts. Abby swallowed hard. She knew he jogged every night, realized it was the reason he was so fit. She ought to have checked with him before coming over.

"Abby, come in." The surprise on Daniel's face was obvious.

"Agnes gave me this bottle of herbal oil for your hands," Abby said quickly. "It's very good for stiffness of any kind."

Daniel's eyebrows rose. "Is it anything like her brews?"

Abby smiled, remembering the morning when she and Daniel had laughed about his illness. "This has no smell," she assured him.

"Great," he said fervently.

The way Abby kept her gaze averted from his bare chest reminded him of the way she had looked when he had asked for help buttoning his shirt. He couldn't resist the temptation to say, "Thank you for bringing the oil over. My hands are very stiff tonight, but maybe I'll be able to use the oil tomorrow night."

She hesitated and Daniel felt a momentary pang for pretending he couldn't rub the oil in himself. He watched the battle that took place in Abby's eyes, before she said, "I...I can massage it into your hands after your run."

"I think I'll take you up on that," said Daniel. "Would you like to come with me?"

"I don't run."

Can't was more like it, thought Abby. Daniel's muscled body made her all the more conscious of the extra weight she carried around. The two buttered rolls she'd eaten at dinner didn't help, either.

"You can ride your bike beside me. Come on, it's a nice night."

It was. Too nice. It was exactly what she was afraid of. Just being near Daniel was enough to fan the spark of awareness within Abby into a blaze. "Not tonight," she said hurriedly. "I have some work to do."

"I'll see you later then."

"Yes."

Daniel tackled his guilt as he jogged. It wasn't fair to use Abby's compassionate nature to get close to her. But he would. Right now it was the only leverage he had. She had gotten under his skin. Her reserve, the pain he glimpsed in her eyes, haunted him. While he tackled the problems The Busy Bee faced, he was going to take on Abby as well.

Daniel hadn't found the best way to bring up the subject of his staying on. One wrong word and she would start avoiding him again. Daniel had always prided himself on his ability to resolve problems. Technical ones.

Dealing with Abby was so different. He felt like a cat tangled up in a ball of yarn. The harder he tried to untangle himself, the worse things became. There was no set formula he could follow, no set results he could expect. He would have to play it by ear, just wait for the right moment. He turned back and headed for Abby.

Abby and her grandmother looked up when the doorbell rang. "Wonder who that could be?" Sarah murmured.

"I'll get it," Abby said, as she went to the door.

She knew who it was even before she checked through the glass peephole. There was only one person who could set her heart beating so frantically.

"It's Daniel," Abby announced over her shoulder as she opened the door.

"Hello, Daniel. Would you like another piece of peach cobbler with a cup of coffee?" Sarah asked, as he entered the family room.

"No cobbler, thank you, but I'll have some coffee if it's not too much trouble," Daniel said quickly. He was eating too much these days.

"No trouble at all." Sarah vanished in the direction of the kitchen before Abby could offer to get the coffee.

"Is this a good time for you to do my hands?" Abby heard Daniel ask above the thumping of her heart.

"Of course."

Sarah handed Daniel a mug of coffee, and said, "Agnes's waiting for me in her room. We're going to look at pictures of her niece's wedding. I'll wish both of you good night."

A small silence followed. Abby didn't know what to say to fill it.

"Were you born on a Friday, Abby?" Daniel's question startled Abby.

"W... Why do you ask?"

"I saw this framed picture in the store today and it had this poem about people born on different days. It said Friday's child is loving and giving and that made me wonder if you were one."

Abby knew the sampler he was talking about. "I was born on a Friday."

Daniel nodded as if he'd expected the answer she'd just given. Abby asked quickly. "What about you? Which day were you born on?"

"Thursday," said Daniel.

" 'Thursday's child has far to go.' " quoted Abby softly.

She wondered if that was why Daniel hadn't put down any roots yet.

Noticing he'd finished his coffee, Abby said, "Would you like me to massage your hands now, Daniel?"

He looked surprised. "I forgot to bring the oil with me. I'll get it right away."

As he hurried to the guest house, Daniel wondered how he could have forgotten the oil. Being absentminded wasn't like him. Neither was the excitement coursing through him. The latter, he supposed, accounted for the former.

When he returned, the family room was empty.

"I won't be a minute," Abby called from the kitchen, above the sound of running water and the clink of dishes.

Daniel looked around the family room as he waited for Abby. Tonight was the first time he had been in this room. Before dinner, Sarah liked to sit in the living room, and he usually left as soon as dinner was over. Earlier he'd told

Sarah he was perfectly fit and he intended taking his turn doing the dishes. Amazingly enough, she'd agreed.

The photo collages on the wall behind the sofa caught Daniel's eye. There were quite a few of them, but the ones of Abby held his attention. There were pictures of her at every age.

"Are these your parents?" he asked without turning around when he heard her enter the room.

Abby stood beside him and looked at the couple in the khaki outfits holding a trio of chimpanzees. The animals had known her parents better than she had. "Yes."

"How did they die?"

"A freak storm in Kenya. They were caught out in it miles from camp. They were so busy observing the chimps, they hadn't noticed the weather."

"I'm sorry."

"I didn't know them." Gramps and Gran had been her real parents. "I was unplanned and my parents had no room in their lives for a baby. They left me with Gran and Gramps when I was a month old, and visited once when I was two. They died when I was four."

Abby talked of them as if they were distant relatives. How different from the relationship he'd had with his parents. "My parents died in a subway accident in New York when I was ten," Daniel said slowly. "I had to go live with my grandparents in Ohio after that."

"That must have been hard on you."

He had never discussed this with anyone else.

"It was. I remember how warm and wonderful our house always seemed. My parents and I did so many things together. For a long time I couldn't believe they would never come back, that they had really left me all alone."

Abby's throat tightened. Though his face remained expressionless, instinct told her Daniel's wound still hadn't healed completely.

"Were you close to your grandparents?" Her own had made all the difference in her life.

"No."

His grandparents had been uncommunicative and cold. Venting his grief over the loss of his parents by bad behavior in school hadn't earned him any points at home, either. The more they punished him, the worse he had become.

Daniel looked at the collage again. A close-up of Abby's face caught his attention. The smile on her lips was carefree, the look of serenity in her eyes an advertisement of the fact that she was happy.

"How old were you when this was taken?"

"Nineteen."

Before she had married the jerk who had robbed her of her self-confidence. Daniel's gaze wandered to the last spot in the collage. It was blank. Had it once held a wedding picture?

Abby tensed as she noticed Daniel's gaze rest on the blank spot. She hadn't replaced the picture of herself in a wedding gown, taken just before she'd left for the church Rod and she had been married in.

"If you'll just sit down here?" she said quickly. She'd become an expert at turning off thoughts of the past. Abby only wished she could turn the pain off as easily.

Daniel seated himself on the sofa, and Abby knelt on the floor in front of him. "Give me your hand." Pouring a teaspoon of oil into her palm she carefully rubbed it all over his hand. Then taking his hand in both of hers she began to massage the palm, working her way upward.

Instantly Abby became aware of heat scorching a path to her brain. Sensing Daniel's gaze on her face, she avoided looking at him. She had done this so many times for so many people. Hamish's bad wrist, Gran's knee. There had never been this eruption of heat before, this feeling that she was walking a tightrope without a net under her.

"Where did you learn to do this?"

Abby barely heard Daniel's question. Without raising her head from her task, she said, "Gran sprained her knee once and it took a long while healing. I watched how the therapist massaged her knee and then I used to do it the same way every night. Agnes gave us a bottle of this oil, and Gran soon recovered completely."

"You've got healing hands."

Daniel's eyes were closed and he looked very relaxed. Abby wondered if Daniel was simply being kind. Gran, Hamish and Agnes were always very kind to her. Abby knew they felt sorry for her. In their own way they wanted to make up to her for the mess she had made of her life. Had Daniel joined the club as well?

Abby jumped when Daniel reached out and touched her shoulder. "Abby, why is it so difficult for you to accept a compliment?"

"I don't know." She did, but she couldn't tell Daniel the reason. Rod.

The bleak note in Abby's voice whipped up Daniel's anger. "You have this low self-image which you cling to as if it's branded on your mind." Cupping her chin, he demanded, "Who did this to you, Abby?"

Her lips felt twice their normal size and her vocal cords were stiff. "I don't know what you mean."

Daniel glanced at the pictures on the wall. "The girl in those pictures didn't lack confidence. Who robbed you of the right to believe in yourself?"

She shook her head. It was impossible to say anything.

Daniel let go of Abby's chin. He wasn't getting through to her. There had to be another way.

As she picked up his other hand and began to massage it, he said, "I started my own business while I was still in college. One of the lecturers kept telling me I would never do well. For a long time I believed what the man said . . . after all he was older, more experienced. He kept bringing the subject up in his class, warning the other students against being in too great a hurry. One day I lost my temper and told him, 'I am going to make it, because I believe in me.' I learned something that day. It didn't matter if anyone else approved of what I did, or not. The only important thing was *I* had to approve of what I did."

Abby didn't say anything as her gaze meshed with Daniel's. "Try it, Abby. Believe in yourself. Have faith in your abilities."

The way Abby looked at him told Daniel he had her complete attention. "You're a wonderful person with so much to offer," he said firmly. "I haven't met anyone else with your capacity for caring for others."

"That isn't hard," Daniel heard Abby mutter.

"You're intelligent and talented." He tried to sound very positive. "Agnes told me you worked as a free-lance interior decorator before you got married. Look at the store, the guest house, this room...they all reflect how good you are. Why did you give up your work, Abby?"

"I wasn't getting any orders."

Rod had told her he wanted his wife to stay home. Rather than argue, she had given in to him. As she always had. By then her growing lack of self-confidence had convinced her she wouldn't be able to make it as an interior decorator anyway.

After Rod's death, Abby had returned to Carbon Canyon. At the back of her mind had been a plan to start her own business again. Once here, she had realized Gran needed her help. Putting what little money she had into the store had been done automatically.

Gran's work was more important than her dreams.

Abby stared at Daniel's hands, her eyes luminous with tears. Daniel wondered if he had trammeled on hurts best forgotten. "When it comes down to it," he said, "each human being has only one cheering section. Ourselves. Think about what I've said, Abby."

She bent her head. He knew he was pushing it, but there was one more thing he had to say. "You're a survivor, Abby."

She looked up, surprised. Daniel felt he had to explain his remark. "The fact you haven't caved in under all your problems, personal or otherwise, proves you're a survivor. Each of us has the spark of survival in us. When things are bad it's up to us to protect that spark till it's strong enough to burn by itself. The only losers are those who let the spark go out."

Enough was enough. Daniel only hoped he hadn't overdone his attempt to restore Abby's self-confidence. Her face was pale and the hand she lifted to cap the bottle of herbal oil shook slightly.

"Thank you for the massage," Daniel said gently. "I'll see you tomorrow."

Upstairs, Abby showered and changed into an embroidered nightie. Settling on the window seat, she drew her knees to her chest. Were all the things Daniel said true? Had she handed Rod the power to bully her, to make her feel she was an idiot?

If she had, it had been because she was so much in love with him. Later it had been because if she ever opposed him, he threw a tantrum. His dark moods lasted for days, and rather than bring one on, she'd preferred to do things his way.

When she had found out about Rod's affairs, Abby knew she should have said something, but by then she blamed herself for the failure of her marriage, believed all the cruel things Rod said. It seemed easier just to continue the way she'd been than cause waves by asking for a divorce.

It hadn't entirely been apathy that had tied her to the marriage. Gran, grieving for Gramps, who had passed away a year after the wedding, would have been tremendously upset by a divorce. Abby had pretended everything was fine between her and Rod on her visits to Carbon Canyon. Deep down in her heart she had never relinquished the hope that they would work through their problems, and everything would become all right one day. Instead, the circumstances surrounding Rod's death had told the whole world what a mess she had made of their marriage. Rod had been returning from an illicit weekend when he and his current lover had been killed.

Take back the power, Abby.

Was it possible to do such a thing? Abby thought of the picture of herself at nineteen. There had been a time when she'd believed in her abilities.

Each of us has the spark of survival in us, Abby. It's up to us to protect it till it's strong enough to burn by itself. You're a survivor.

She had to get off the bleachers where she had spent so much time watching life pass her by. There was only one way to find out if she could really regain control of her life. Abby knew she had to test what Daniel had told her.

Only time would tell if he was right.

Chapter Six

At the end of his third week, Daniel stepped into the community room to find Hamish bent over the wooden stork. The smooth, artistic lines of the bird testified to Hamish's talent and Daniel's lack of it.

"Good morning, Mr. McArthur."

"Ah, Daniel, come in." Hamish looked up from his carving and actually smiled. "Sarah tells me you've decided to extend your stay with us."

"Well . . ." Daniel didn't know what to say. "I haven't really done anything to help the store. The billboard and the flyers have brought in a few more customers but that isn't enough to get The Busy Bee back on its feet."

"Glad you're staying," Hamish said with more geniality than he had ever exhibited before. "Maybe we'll make a whittler of you yet."

That would be the day. Daniel thought of the lopsided object his carving had yielded and a corner of his mouth lifted. He had changed considerably since he'd come here, but there were some things that could never change. One was his whittling abilities.

In the office, Abby tensed. Why hadn't Daniel mentioned his decision to stay on to her? She hadn't seen much of him this week. Jack Williams was growing steadily weaker, and she had been spending all her free time at St. Michael's.

A few minutes later she looked up as Daniel entered the office. "Hi!"

She'd forgotten the effect that half smile of his had on her, the way the lines around his eyes crinkled.

"I'm just cleaning up," she said quickly, noticing the surprised look on his face. "I'll be out of your way in five minutes."

Daniel's gaze fell to the drawer she had placed on top of the desk. It was the one with the photographs. Half-empty.

"Want some coffee?" he asked casually, holding up the cup he had poured himself in the community room.

"No thanks."

Watching as Abby dumped the rest of the pictures into a large envelope he said cautiously, "I'm going to be here awhile longer."

Their gazes linked.

"I know," said Abby. "I heard you tell Hamish just now."

And she wasn't asking him why?

"I feel there has to be more I can do to help The Busy Bee. Your grandmother, Agnes, Hamish and all the others, they work so hard. They deserve to succeed."

Abby's face showed the surprise she felt.

"I'm sorry about my attitude toward them in the beginning, Abby. I was raised by grandparents who were very strict and I've always associated any older person with them.

I was wrong. More and more I'm learning generalizations don't work. Not in business, not in life."

It was a very generous apology.

"Your grandmother and her friends are so warm and affectionate," Daniel continued. "I hope I haven't hurt anybody's feelings."

It was Abby's turn to be surprised. "What makes you think you might have hurt anyone?"

"I'm always refusing their offers of help. I don't mix much. I've never found it easy to talk to any of them, except Sarah and Agnes. For a long time I blamed my grandparents for the way I am. Now I realize the way I am has nothing to do with them. It has to do with me."

"Why did you blame your grandparents?"

"They were so different from my parents. I used to wonder if they cared for me at all. We rarely talked to each other. I know I wasn't an easy boy to get along with, but I missed my mother and father so much."

Abby's heart twisted at the thought of the lonely ten-year-old. "Hamish told me once that his parents never talked of their emotions, and he grew up thinking a man's way of telling his family he loved them was providing for them. Maybe your grandparents were like that too."

Trust Abby to make excuses for everybody. "Maybe."

"It couldn't have been easy on them losing their son and daughter-in-law. Did you talk to them about how you felt?" Abby asked.

"No." Daniel tossed his empty cup in the trash can.

Shock over his parents' death had changed to anger. Rage had taken the form of rebellion. No one had been able to cross the moat he'd built around himself.

"Being here has made me realize how difficult I made things for them. I wish I had a chance to go back, to apologize, but life's a one-way street. Maybe finding a way to help Sarah and her friends is my way of working through this guilt I harbor.''

Abby nodded as if she understood and Daniel went on, ''I called them once a month after I left home. The conversations we had never lasted long. We didn't know what to say to each other.''

His stay here had made him understand how lonely old people were. The thought he should have done more for his grandparents weighed heavily on him.

''You cared enough to keep in touch,'' Abby pointed out.

''Yes, but I wish I had told them I loved them, just once. Eve was right about me.''

Abby held her breath.

''She said I was cold.''

Abby's heart began to race. She could understand how hard communication had been for Daniel and his grandparents. She couldn't understand how Daniel could believe a completely false accusation.

''You aren't cold.'' There was no shred of doubt in Abby's voice. ''You wouldn't have given us so much of your vacation time if you were. There are very few people Hamish, Agnes and Gran trust, but you're definitely one of them.''

''They're good for my ego.''

Daniel's tone told Abby he wasn't completely convinced. Touched by the glimpse she got of the lonely boy behind the reserved man, Abby blinked the tears from her eyes. Daniel wasn't cold.

Walking around the desk, she reached for both his hands. As he looked at her in surprise, she stood on tiptoe and placed her mouth against his. Warmly, sweetly, she kissed him.

Heat melted surprise. Wrapping his arms around her, Daniel dragged her closer. Gentleness gave way to hunger as

Abby's mouth opened under his. Lifting one hand Daniel threaded it through Abby's hair.

Abby loved the feeling of Daniel's back under her hands. Loved matching the demands his mouth made with some of her own.

There was no room for thought till the need for air made them pause. Daniel looked at Abby's face and saw the elation fade, as embarrassment took its place.

"That was just to prove you aren't cold," she said breathlessly. Moving away from him, she went behind the desk.

Trust Abby to think of the quickest, most thorough way of making her point. The kiss reminded him of the way she had challenged him at the seminar. Abby's shortcuts may be unusual, but they were very effective.

"I get the message." Daniel's gaze was still on her mouth.

Had proving a point been all it was? He wanted to kiss Abby again, feel that wonderful mouth under his.

Picking up the envelope on the desk, Abby said, "I have to help in the store."

"I'd better get on with my work." Daniel couldn't keep the reluctance out of his voice.

For a long time after Abby left, he sat doodling on a pad. *Can't complain of emptiness now, can you, Hawthorn?*

No, he couldn't. His life was filled with emotions and questions. He had changed so much. Looking at everything from a different perspective had broadened the scope of his experiences. He wanted different things now. To help Abby, to get the store back on its feet, to make amends for the past.

Daniel wondered if he had helped himself to more than he would ever be able to deal with.

Talking to Abby about his relationship with his grandparents had eased the load of bitterness he had carried around for so long. If he'd been cold with Eve, it was because he'd held a part of himself back from her. Since his parents' death he'd held a part of himself back from everyone. He was afraid of loving too much, afraid of losing those he loved.

His work had become a nice safe wall to hide behind.

Take back the power, Abby.

Daniel's words echoed and re-echoed in her mind, as Abby stepped into Lou Nelson's printing shop on Main Street.

"Hello, Abby." Lou greeted her with a hug. "I never thought I'd see the Saturday you'd get away from the store. Does Sarah need more flyers?"

Abby shook her head. "No. This is for me. I need some business cards and flyers for my interior-decorating business."

Lou beamed at her. "Why, I'm happy you're going to have another shot at it, Abby. Everyone praises the way you did my parlor. They can't believe how little it cost. I just know you're going to be great at it. How many business cards and flyers would you like?"

Abby had done Lou's parlor when she'd come home from college one year, during summer vacation. She had been very young and very excited about her work in those days.

"Five hundred, please." It didn't hurt to dream big. Abby hesitated and then said, "I thought I'd distribute them to half the homes in the new developments, see what happens and then have some more printed."

"That's a great idea. It'll take a day to get them ready. I know some teenagers who will do the legwork for you. They charge on an hourly basis."

"That'll help. Thanks, Lou."

Abby showed Lou the design she'd thought up for her business cards and the idea for her flyer. It was a while before their business discussion ended.

"I have to go now," Abby said. "I have a few things to pick up for Jack Williams."

"Oh, I almost forgot." Lou opened a drawer and took out a packet. "Katy sent pictures of the baby, and said to be sure and give you one. After all our planning, he had to be born when I wasn't there."

Abby looked at the pictures of the baby boy and said, "He's adorable. I love the name Nathan. I'll call Katy tonight."

Picking out a picture, she thanked Lou and said goodbye.

Outside the store she paused and took a deep breath. It was hard to imagine Katy as a mother. Her friend had been the tomboyish type who'd said she wanted to be president of a company. Abby had been the one who'd always said she wanted a husband and children. Only Rod hadn't wanted any.

If she'd had a baby, things would have been different after Rod's death. She would have avoided the intense bouts of loneliness that gripped her from time to time. Now, it was too late.

"Hi, Abby!"

She looked straight into Daniel's eyes and then around her. She was blocking the way to Lou's store by standing here daydreaming.

"Is something wrong?"

Hoping he hadn't seen the tears in her eyes, Abby shook her head. She had decided to make a new beginning. Brooding over what-might-have-been wasn't part of her plan.

She smiled at Daniel. "I'm fine. I'll see you back at the house. I have a few more errands to run."

"Right." Daniel stood aside to let Abby pass before entering the store. He'd wondered about the look on her face, but with Abby he knew better than to insist she tell him what was wrong.

"Things have changed so much since you came to Carbon Canyon," Lou told Daniel as she handed him the business cards he had ordered for himself. "You've made a difference in such a short time. What is it? Two weeks?"

"Three." Today made it exactly that. "I haven't done much."

"Helping Sarah and the others save that store is a gift to the whole community. Some of us would be very lonely if we couldn't meet there. You read about people like us. Some of us are just lonesome but others are the real shut-ins, and it's more than sad. They're afraid to go out. They have no one to talk to. It must be a terrible feeling."

"I'm glad Abby asked me to come here."

Daniel knew how important the store was to the people in Carbon Canyon.

"I'm giving you these cards at cost," Lou told him. "I'll be happy to help with anything else you want done."

Her tone encouraged Daniel to ask his next question. "Have you known Abby long?"

"Sarah and I raised Abby and my Katy together. I just showed Abby pictures of Katy's baby boy. The look on her face almost broke my heart."

Daniel felt his stomach tighten. Why had Abby looked sad? She would make a wonderful mother.

Lou's words seemed to answer his questions. "I don't know if she'll ever be able to trust any man again. That Rod was a no-good scoundrel."

"Thanks for the cards, Lou." Daniel took the package and left the store.

Outside he stood in much the same place Abby had, and gazed down Main Street. Abby and children. Pictures whirled in his brain, teasing him. Babies with green eyes and that black hair. Children who, like their mother, would care about people and causes.

Abby closed the menu and set it beside her plate. The chicken salad had been a wise decision. It wasn't only in the area of her work that she wanted to take control. She had to do it with her eating habits as well. Abby didn't expect overnight success with her diet. She would take losing weight one step at a time, try planning her meals better.

Another thing to work on was managing her time better. She'd have to learn to keep some of it for herself without feeling guilty. It wasn't going to be easy.

Three days after the flyers were all distributed, Abby received her first call. The woman on the other end of the line had just bought a house in Canyon Crest Estates. She wanted to know when Abby could meet with her.

Abby's voice wouldn't function, and her legs began to shake. She'd seen the model homes in Canyon Crest Estates. The houses were all five-hundred-thousand dollars and up. Decorating a big house was a dream come true, but what if she made a mess of it? What if...

You can do anything you want, Abby.

The ring of assurance in Daniel's voice as he had said the words spliced through Abby's panic. "Mrs. Greggory? I'm free at six this evening. Would that suit you?"

Abby spent the rest of the day organizing. Digging out the album that held photographs of some of the best designs she'd done, she found a magazine that had pictures of the latest fashions in window treatments. Next she hunted for something businesslike and confidence-building to wear. Thanks to Agnes, Abby had plenty of clothes.

Halfway down the stairs on her way to the store for a box of chocolates, Abby stopped. No, she wasn't going that route again. She had to stop reaching for food every time she was under stress. Changing direction she went into the kitchen and found some carrot sticks. As she munched on them, Abby thought of the turn her life had taken. The golden glow of her expectations had become a canvas to paint dreams on. Hope that everything would turn out well for The Busy Bee provided a splash of green. Her love for Gran was a deep, rich blue. Hamish, Agnes, Jack Williams, Lou and all her other friends were a warm, comforting pink. Daniel . . . Abby's breath caught in her throat . . . Daniel was the red of excitement, of danger that she couldn't resist.

"Where's Abby?" Daniel asked Sarah Trenton casually. He had looked for her in the office, in the community room, the house. As a last resort he was trying the store.

Sarah looked up from the cash register. "She had to go out."

"I see," said Daniel.

He'd expected this after the kiss. Abby had avoiding him down to a fine art. Was she out as in out shopping, out helping someone, or out taking a perfectly healthy Muffy on yet another trip to the vet? Unable to ask the questions he picked up a cushion, put it down, wandered down an aisle and stared blankly at a quilt.

What's the matter with you, Hawthorn?

He couldn't explain the feeling gripping him, the longing to be with Abby.

"Abby said she was going to Canyon Crest Estates to look into the possibility of decorating someone's house."

Daniel spun around. The smile on Sarah Trenton's face told him she had tuned into the cause of his restlessness.

"It was something you said that convinced her to give her business another try. Thank you, Daniel."

Sarah's eyes conveyed an unspoken message to Daniel. *I owe you for helping Abby back to this point, but hurt her and you'll have to reckon with me.*

Daniel had a pretty good idea Sarah wouldn't be the only one he'd have to deal with. There was Agnes and Hamish and ninety percent of Carbon Canyon watching out for Abby.

He should be happy that Abby had decided to give his suggestions a try. As for the restlessness...maybe he needed some time alone to think about it. Time away from Carbon Canyon.

On impulse he decided to go to Los Angeles. In the world he was used to, everything here would probably take on a different perspective.

Telling Sarah he was going to Los Angeles and would be back in time for the weekly meeting the next day only took a minute. Daniel hurried to the guest house for his car keys. He'd made the right decision. It was time to touch base with his world again.

"Gran, I can't believe it." Abby walked into the house, her cheeks fire-engine red. "The Greggorys' place is huge and so beautiful. It will take a miracle to land the contract. Mrs. G. and I talked, and she asked me to submit an estimate."

Sarah smiled at her granddaughter. "I know you'll get the job, Abby."

Abby chuckled. If she'd told Gran she was putting in a bid for redecorating the White House, the comment would have been the same.

"How are things at the store?" Abby asked.

"Everything's fine. Daniel stopped by to find out where you were."

"He did?" Abby's gaze fell on the bottle of oil on the mantelpiece.

Her grandmother looked in the same direction. "He mentioned how much better his hands are feeling, and I noticed at dinner he was finding it easier to bend his fingers over his fork and knife."

Abby set her enormous patchwork bag down. "I'll give him a massage after dinner."

"Oh." Sarah peered at her crocheting. "Daniel won't be here for dinner. He's gone to Los Angeles."

"Los Angeles?"

Abby couldn't believe it. Her mouth went dry. What had prompted the sudden decision to leave?

"Only for the night. He'll be back tomorrow."

"I see."

The rush of relief coursing through Abby left her weak. For the few seconds when she had thought Daniel had left for good, she'd felt as if someone had switched off all the lights and left her in the dark.

The fact that he had gone to Los Angeles had her on edge. Was he missing the bright lights, or was there someone special he couldn't do without?

Sarah smiled as Abby left the room. Her granddaughter's reaction to the news when she'd heard Daniel had gone to L.A. was just what Sarah had hoped for. So was the way Daniel had looked this morning.

It was just like David, Sarah's husband, had always said. "Life isn't all up or all down. It's like a Ferris wheel. Sometimes you're right on top and at others you're at the bottom. When you're at the bottom, all you have to do is be patient till it's your turn to be on top again."

Sarah was glad Abby was finally on the upswing.

"Hi!" One quick look showed Daniel the community room was empty except for Abby whittling her dog in the corner. A glance at the clock showed it was barely seven. What was she doing here at this time?

"Hi!" She gave him a startled look. "You must have left L.A. very early."

"Five." He had tossed and turned all night. An early start back seemed to be the best idea he'd had in the last twenty-four hours.

His suite at the Castilian had seemed as sterile as an operating room in a hospital. Daniel had missed falling asleep to the sound of owls calling to each other in the woods and being woken by the sounds of birds. He had missed the warmth of Abby's presence, missed sitting at Sarah's dinner table and listening to an account of everyone's day. Ordinary things. *Important* things.

Realizing Abby wasn't going to say anything, Daniel asked, "How did your meeting go yesterday?"

There was a glow in Abby's eyes as she looked at him. "Very well. I've been asked to submit an estimate."

It was just what she needed.

"I stayed up half the night thinking about Mrs. G.'s house," Abby said quickly as her eyes met Daniel's. "I woke up early and knew I had to come down here and do something else just to calm down. I still can't believe it."

She didn't want to admit, even to herself, that part of her sleeplessness had to do with Daniel's absence. The rush of joy she'd experienced when he walked into the room was still with her.

"There's something I wanted to talk to you about before the meeting," Daniel said.

"Yes?"

"The accounts show the store has reached a break-even point."

Abby knew that the next two weeks might not be enough to show a profit large enough to make this month's payment.

"Do you think...?" she began, but the hope in her voice died at the look on Daniel's face.

"You don't think we'll make it, do you?"

Daniel shook his head. "Not unless we double our business or you let me lend you some money for next month's payment."

He knew the answer to his offer already, but the suggestion had been worth a try.

"We cannot continue to borrow money we have no way of repaying. We'll have to foreclose. I don't know how to tell G... Gran and the others the news."

Daniel hated the tremor of disappointment in Abby's voice. Hated the fact he'd failed. It no longer mattered that his integrity was in question. All he wanted was to help Abby. He'd spent part of last night wondering what he could do to turn things around for The Busy Bee.

"Don't tell them yet. I have an idea that just might work. I met someone last night who might help us."

"What idea and who?" Abby asked.

"A friend of mine, Hank Trammell, is an editor at the *Times*. We shared our first apartment together in college. Bumping into him in the Castilian was sheer chance. He was just leaving after a big publicity bash for a presidential candidate when I arrived. We had dinner together and I mentioned the store."

Daniel held his breath, waiting for Abby to say something. When she didn't he proceeded carefully. "Hank expressed interest in doing an article on The Busy Bee."

"We're not important, or successful."

"You're unusual," said Daniel firmly, not sure if he meant Abby or the business. "Hank said he hadn't heard of entrepreneurship with such a unique slant in a long time. An article in the *Times* could get you more publicity than you'll ever need."

He saw hope kindle in Abby's eyes again. "Do you think it'll work?"

Daniel glanced at his watch. "We can give it a try if you don't think—" He stopped.

"Think what?" asked Abby.

"Think I'm exploiting the trio or something."

Abby stared at him. Daniel had grounds for his doubts. She had been as protective as a mother tigress when he'd first arrived.

"I don't think you are capable of exploiting anyone," Abby said, "especially the trio. You care about them."

"Shall I call Hank and find out if he still wants to come?"

"Yes, please."

As Daniel left the room, Abby went back to her whittling. Last night she had received a warning. Daniel's time here was limited. They were from two entirely different worlds. Their paths had collided for a while, but things would eventually go back to the way they had been.

Abby's heart contracted at the thought. Daniel was being very kind about helping them, but he must be impatient to get back to his own life. He couldn't carry them and their problems around forever.

The sharp crack made her jump. Abby stared at the dog she was working on. She had broken the blade of her knife. Throwing it into a trash can, Abby decided the sooner Daniel left Carbon Canyon the sooner life would return to normal.

Daniel returned as she took a new knife out of Hamish's drawer. "Hank says he's tossed the idea around with some of his colleagues. Everyone likes the idea of doing an article on The Busy Bee. He's coming down here tomorrow."

"So soon?"

Daniel must have really pulled strings to get someone as important as an editor at the *Times* to come down at a moment's notice. On the other hand it could be because the sooner he got things sorted out here, the sooner Daniel could get back to Los Angeles.

"Hank says he's going to have the article out in this Sunday's edition. That's how keen he is on it. People are tired of constantly hearing about the recession and the poor economy. This is something really positive, and he feels it will have far-reaching results. Human-interest stories always do."

Abby tried to smile. Getting what she wanted so badly meant losing Daniel.

"I'd better tell Gran and the others." There was never any question that the work Gran was doing here was more important than Abby's muddled feelings.

Daniel nodded. "I've already had breakfast. I'll be in the guest house if you need me."

He'd barely slept last night. That must be why he had imagined the sadness in Abby's eyes.

The sight of her in the white skirt and sweater had convinced him going to Los Angeles had been an absolute waste of his time.

Daniel looked at the portable computer he'd brought back with him. He planned to start working out ideas for his next book. Work might accomplish something nothing else could these days. It might shut out thoughts of Abby.

A couple of hours later, Daniel got up from his desk and walked over to the window. He frowned. It looked as if someone had set up a housecleaning movie set in the yard. Hamish was on a ladder checking the drains, Sarah had her hair tied up in a scarf and was carrying a small pail of water. Agnes was sweeping the drive while a few others were clipping the hedges.

"What's happening?" Daniel enquired, stepping out of the guest house.

"Daniel," Sarah called. "We won't be able to have the meeting today."

"Why not?"

"We have to get the place cleaned up for your friend from the *Times*."

"But the place is clean enough," Daniel said.

Sarah looked at him in surprise. "Of course it isn't. Now, let me get on with my work."

Daniel decided to go in search of Abby. He found her in the store, washing the front window.

"The store is perfectly clean," Daniel said, feeling guilty about all the work he had created.

"Of course, it isn't." Abby used exactly the same tone Sarah had.

Sighing, Daniel climbed into the window. If you couldn't beat them, you may as well join them. It was one of Sarah's sayings that fit this occasion perfectly.

"Shall I do this side?" he asked.

Abby paused in her scrubbing. "You don't have to help."

"I know I don't *have* to help," Daniel asserted. "Is it okay if I help because I *want* to?"

"I guess."

Five minutes later, Abby looked over her shoulder. The side of the window Daniel was working in was spotless. Turning around, she looked at him.

He didn't seem to mind helping. In fact, Daniel looked as if he belonged here.

Abby's heart missed a beat. That line of thinking brought nothing but trouble.

Three hours later, Daniel looked around the store. Everything had been taken off the shelves. The shelves had been wiped down and the merchandise rearranged. For the last half hour Abby had kept changing things around.

"I'm done," she announced at last.

Daniel stretched his hands overhead, trying to get the kinks out of his back. "This place would pass a white-glove inspection," he said. "I didn't know you were such a fanatic about cleanliness."

Abby looked at him and the color in her face faded. "I'm sorry," she said stiffly.

"I meant it as a joke." Daniel cursed himself. "The place looks beautiful."

Abby turned away and began picking up the rags and polish they had used. Daniel wondered what he could say to set things right.

"Rod said I was never satisfied because I was a perfectionist. He said even a saint wouldn't please me."

Anger filled Daniel at Abby's words. He looked around the store, and then said slowly, "That is a matter of opinion. I think the world needs more people who care enough to do their work really well. We have plenty who do barely enough to get by."

Abby looked at Daniel. His words healed her emotional wounds. This is what she would miss the most when he left. His way of making her feel good about herself. Abby looked at him and saw the light in his eyes change. Daniel took a step forward and her heart began to race.

"Lunch is ready."

Abby told herself Hamish's voice over the intercom was a welcome interruption.

Chapter Seven

Hank Trammell arrived at ten the next morning with a photographer and an assistant. Daniel noticed Abby kept well out of camera range and left it to the trio and their friends to do all the talking.

"How's it going?" he asked Hank after a while.

"Great. This is even better than I hoped for. I'm going to do a centerspread. Our readers are going to love it. There's just one thing...."

"What?" This had turned out better than anything Daniel had ever expected.

"Introduce me to the granddaughter, will you? She's a real looker."

Daniel's head snapped around and his mouth tightened. "Abby's not available," he said curtly.

"Oh, ho! Do I detect a note of jealousy here? Has the invincible Daniel Hawthorn fallen in love at last?"

Someone called to Hank and he turned away with a grin. Daniel stalked off in the direction of the office.

Had Hank been right about the jealousy? Remembering the urge to take his friend by the neck and throw him against the wall, Daniel wondered what was wrong with him. He had no claim on Abby.

Abby glanced at the picnic table covered with food. Gran had insisted on serving refreshments out here to Hank Trammel and his men.

Eyeing the iced tea in the jug, Abby decided to replenish it. Everyone seemed to want some.

"Ah, Ms. Silver. Just the person I wanted to have a word with."

Abby looked up in surprise as Hank fell into step beside her. He asked her a few questions about the store, and then said, "Is Daniel planning on staying here long?"

"I don't know." She hoped he would, but a month had already gone by. Daniel had four weeks left of his vacation.

"Tell me," said Hank casually, "do you ever come up to L.A.? If you do, I'd like to meet you for lunch."

Amazed, Abby looked at Hank. Why was he inviting her to lunch?

"I'm really busy right now with the store and my interior-decorating business."

"Pity." Was it her imagination or did the editor actually look disappointed? "I'll give you my card, and if you change your mind, give me a call."

"I thought that went very well," Sarah said that night at dinner. "What did your friend think, Daniel?"

"He wants to do a centerspread of the article in the People section."

"He also wants Abby to go out with him." Everyone looked at Agnes in surprise and she said quickly, "I just came into the house for an aspirin, and I heard them talking in the kitchen."

Abby couldn't stop herself blushing. What on earth was the matter with Agnes, blurting out something like that?

Daniel looked at his plate. He should have punched Hank when he'd had the chance.

"I think he's a very nice young man," Sarah said. "He asked me a great many questions about you, Abby. Come to think of it, he asked more questions about you than the store."

Daniel's hand tightened over the fork.

"He's single and a bachelor," said Hamish. "I talked to him and he's quite well-to-do."

Abby knew exactly what they were up to. "If you'll excuse me," she said, picking up her plate, "I have work to do."

"Hank struck me as a patient sort," said Sarah, after Abby left. "I think he'll get her to change her mind about going out with him."

"Definitely," said Agnes.

"Excuse me," Daniel said abruptly. "It's been a long day. I think I'll take Princess and Muffy for a run and turn in early."

There was only so much a man could take.

As soon as the front door closed, Sarah and Agnes turned to Hamish in surprise.

"Never thought we'd see the day you'd help us," Sarah said.

"Well." Hamish shrugged as he helped himself to another piece of pie. "I like Daniel. He'll never make a whittler, but he's all right."

As he concentrated on the pie, the two women exchanged smug, we-knew-that-all-along looks.

In her room, Abby stood by the window. Why had Hank asked her to go out? She hadn't been mistaken about the gleam of interest in his eyes or the disappointment when she'd said she couldn't go.

She wasn't the least bit interested in Hank Trammell, but being asked out by him had done wonders for her ego. Abby turned to the triple mirror on her dresser, searching for what Hank had seen in her. All she saw was a reflection of Daniel's disapproving face as he glared at her across the dining table.

"Wonder what's gotten into him," Abby murmured, as she sat at the writing table in her room. She had a collection of magazines to go through in her search for ideas for Mrs. G.'s new house.

The house had more glass than wall. Drapes would be the biggest expense. Looking over the measurements she'd taken when Mrs. G. had asked her to submit an estimate, Abby wondered if she should check out the outlet plaza in Carbon Canyon as well. If they had what she wanted, delivery would be quicker and cost less.

It was going to take her one day to verify prices, another to come up with her bid. It was a good thing she had agreed to Gran and Agnes's suggestion that she take the next couple of days off from the store to concentrate on getting her bid ready.

Daniel pushed himself harder than ever as he ran, but he couldn't get away from his thoughts.

He wanted Abby. The thought that someone else might think her as attractive as he did, irked him. What if Abby preferred Hank Trammell to him? What had Sarah said? Hank was just right for Abby. Trammell was all the things Daniel was not. Patient, kind, fun loving.

Daniel shook his head. Abby didn't belong to him. He had no right to be so angry about what had happened.

Daniel ran faster into the night.

* * *

Preparing the estimate was more frightening than Abby had anticipated. The day she'd spent in L.A. had been fun. Discovering she hadn't lost her knack for spotting a bargain had made her feel good.

The feeling had lasted till today. Throughout the morning, she found herself taking frequent breaks to worry. The band of anxiety around her chest tightened as the hours passed. By mid-morning, she wasn't sure she could handle the job even if she got it.

When she couldn't stand it a minute longer, Abby went downstairs. Hamish had been baking, and a tray of enormous chocolate-chip cookies stood on the kitchen counter. Abby poured herself a glass of milk. Placing two cookies on a plate, she carried it over to the kitchen table.

Doubts lapped against the edges of her mind, eroding her new resolutions. Mrs. G.'s house was very big. Too big for her to handle. Why couldn't someone have called her with a small job? What if she did everything, and Mrs. G. didn't like it?

It was easy for Daniel to talk about being in control. Talking was one thing. Doing it quite another. She would never get the hang of it.

A little later, Abby looked from her plate to the tray on the counter. Six giant cookies were gone.

It was the last straw. She couldn't do a single thing right. Not even controlling what she ate.

Before she could stop them, tears rolled down her cheeks, and she was sobbing. She would never be anything but a good-natured, well mannered failure.

Daniel entered the kitchen and stopped dead at the sight of Abby crying her heart out. "What's wrong?"

Abby seemed to cry even harder at the sight of him. "Wh... What are you doing here?" she asked.

"Hamish asked me to fetch the cookies," said Daniel.

"I've—I've eaten half of them," sobbed Abby.

Was that why she was so upset?

"There are still plenty here," Daniel pointed out. "Want to tell me what's really bothering you?"

Abby plucked a tissue out of the box on the counter and blew her nose. "I can't stay in control," she said defiantly. "I don't have the power. I never will."

Daniel bit back a smile. Abby sounded as if believing in oneself was nothing more than the wish to do so. "It isn't something that can be acquired overnight. Is the thought of doing the bid for Mrs. G.'s house scaring you?"

"Yes. I know she won't give me the contract. I have very little experience, and hardly any references."

"Have you got the estimate ready?"

"No," said Abby. "It's no use."

Daniel leaned against the counter. "Isn't that for Mrs. G. to decide?" he asked. "Your part is merely to get it ready and give it to her, not anticipate her refusal. In business you have to hope for the best."

"What if I make a mess of decorating her house and she doesn't like it? What if she sues me for ruining her five-hundred-thousand-dollar house?" The hiccup that followed the words had Daniel clenching his hands.

"What if she loves it and a dozen of her friends call you asking you to redo their houses?" he demanded. "What if someone sees your work and decides you're good enough to do an office building, or a private clinic?"

Abby stared at him in silence.

"Every situation has more than one angle," he pointed out. "You have to consider them all."

Daniel's words were like a foothold in the slippery well of her misgivings. Part of the lump in Abby's throat dissolved. He was right, as usual.

"I'm not big in the confidence department." Abby's voice sounded dismal. "Do you think developing the power improves with practise?"

Daniel fought the urge to take Abby into his arms. He'd thought her a failure at their first meeting. These past few weeks had shown him how wrong first impressions could be. She may not know it but she was a fighter.

"You don't have to be a certain type to be successful. Just be yourself, Abby."

Abby sniffed.

"About being in control," Daniel went on casually, "it's done bit by bit, over a lifetime. I can't say I'm in complete control of my life yet. I haven't met anyone who can claim that."

Abby reached for another tissue as Daniel said, "Everyone slips back sometimes. The important thing is to get back on track, not to give up trying. It's what life is all about."

Put like that, it seemed trying was the least she could do. "I guess I should finish getting the estimate ready."

"Abby," Daniel called as she was at the kitchen door. Abby turned to look at him, hoping he hadn't noticed how red her nose was. "You're not a coward, or a quitter. If you were, The Busy Bee wouldn't be where it is today."

You're not a coward or a quitter.

Abby hugged the words to her as she worked through the afternoon. The fact that Daniel believed in her strengthened Abby's belief in herself. He had a knack for making everything seem so simple.

Abby woke early Sunday morning, dressed quickly and went downstairs to wait for the morning paper. It was barely six o'clock, and the paper was delivered around seven, but she couldn't stay in bed any longer.

Letting the dogs out of the run, she watched them race into the woods at the back of the house.

Would the publicity help pull The Busy Bee out of the red once and for all? So far this month they only had half the money ready for their next mortgage payment. They still owed Daniel for four months.

Mrs. G.'s advance, if Abby got the job, would help make next month's payment.

"Hi!"

"Hi!" Abby looked at Daniel. In blue jeans and a yellow T-shirt he looked as if he'd dressed in a hurry. "What are you doing up so early?"

"Thought I'd wait for the paper with you."

"We could have picked up an edition at the store last night, but I've been so busy with Mrs. G.'s work I didn't remember it till too late."

"You've finished the bid?"

Abby nodded shyly. "Thanks to you."

"No, Abby." Daniel's voice sounded perfectly serious. "You did this, not me."

Abby looked at him. In the early morning light Daniel seemed sexier than ever. Her heart began to pound.

"You've helped us so much since you've come here," she said. "I don't know what we would have done without you."

"You've all helped me," said Daniel. "More than I can tell. I was out of touch with a part of myself. I had begun to think there was no more to life than making money and success. Here, I've managed to find that part, make a few important decisions."

"I'm glad."

She would miss him badly.

As his gaze met Abby's, Daniel's eyes widened.

"Remember those signals I told you about that a man and a woman send out to each other?"

Abby nodded.

"Well, I'm receiving them now from you."

His hands were on her shoulders. Abby had no idea of moving closer to him, but she must have, because their mouths met and the rest of the world went out of focus.

Neither of them noticed the boy cycle up the drive, or the paper whizz past them. The thump as it hit the porch made Abby draw away.

She looked at Daniel in a daze, wondering why kissing him felt so right. And so wonderful. The glint in his eyes made her blood run wild and hot.

"The paper," he reminded her.

"The paper," Abby agreed reluctantly.

As Abby and Daniel went into the kitchen, the others joined them. Hank Trammell had done them proud. The article was all he had promised, and more. The pictures were beautiful.

"This is wonderful," Sarah said.

"I think this is going to do the trick for us." Daniel's gaze was fixed on Abby. He couldn't mistake the signals he was getting now. She hadn't looked at him once since they had come in. "Be prepared to be very busy from now on."

As the others talked in the background, Daniel thought back to the kiss. What had gone wrong? Abby had definitely given it her all. Recalling the way she had wrapped her arms around him and matched his enthusiasm, he wondered why she was backing off now.

Abby couldn't understand the way she had responded to Daniel. Uninhibited, wild, *hot*. She wanted more. Her self-control was in shreds and it didn't even matter.

The only thing that bothered her was what did Daniel want? She stole a quick look at him. He seemed as composed as ever as he talked to Gran. The kiss hadn't affected him at all. She had to make sure she didn't embarrass Daniel with the way she felt, had to remember he would be gone soon.

Give her time, Hawthorn.

It was obvious, Daniel told himself later, that Abby wasn't ready to discuss her feelings. Rushing her would only frighten her. He had to find some way to tell her how he felt. A way that wouldn't send her back into her shell.

Daniel went in search of Agnes that afternoon. He found her in the community room reading a magazine.

"Do you have some red thread I can sew this on with?" he asked, holding out the button that he had pulled off his shirt.

Agnes looked at the button and said, "Leave it on my table, and I'll do it later. What you need is a wife to take care of such tasks for you. Why aren't you married?"

"I've been too involved in my work," Daniel said hesitantly.

"Abby is a nice person." Agnes never wasted time getting to the point.

"Yes, she is," Daniel said quietly. "How did she meet her late husband?"

Maybe he could find some what-not-to-do clues if he knew a little more of what had happened.

"At Katy Nelson's wedding. Sarah had the reception here because Lou has a very small yard. Rod took one look at Abby and this place, decided she had money, and swept her off her feet. He didn't find out till too late that the money Abby's parents left her was in trust, and Abby wouldn't get it till she was twenty-five. By then it was too late."

Abby, Daniel decided, would be wary of any sudden moves. He'd have to take it very slow, and try to curb his impatience.

In spite of what Daniel had said, no one could believe the deluge of mail they received in the course of the week. Since Monday, the store had been inundated with customers. Gran had asked two of her friends to help out.

"There are checks, offers from corporations to sponsor us, orders for the things we make, requests for catalogs. One person writes he's here on holiday from France and would it be possible for us to mail lace curtains to his home address." Sarah's flushed cheeks and sparkling eyes made her look twenty years younger. "If this is a dream, don't wake me up."

Daniel looked around the community room. Agnes opened the letters and sorted them into piles. Hamish made a note of all the checks they'd received. Sarah read aloud from some of the letters. The store had closed an hour ago.

Daniel looked at Abby. She sat back from the group, watching him. He could have sworn there was pain in her eyes. As their gazes met, she got up, excused herself and left the room.

Daniel stood to go after her, just as Hamish held a letter out to him. "Look at this one, will you? It's from an eighty-five-year-old man who wants to leave us all his money."

Daniel sat again, trying to mask his uneasiness. What was wrong with Abby? The outcome was exactly what she had wanted, wasn't it?

That thought was running through Abby's head as well. One of Gran's favorite sayings was, Be careful what you want. You may get it.

Abby was very familiar with the message behind the words. She had wanted The Busy Bee to pull through. Her pleasure over the success they'd met with was shadowed by the thought that Daniel would soon be leaving them. There was no longer any need for him to stay on in Carbon Canyon.

Thursday night, Daniel stepped into the office and found Abby looking at some papers.

"Hi! I saw the light and wondered who was in here this late." He hadn't seen her all of yesterday. Sarah had mentioned Abby was spending the day with Jack Williams at St. Michael's. She hadn't shown up at Hamish's class, either. Daniel had taken his frustration out by knocking chips off his block of wood.

"Abby, what's wrong?" Daniel had meant to lead up to it gradually, but the look on her face destroyed the little patience he'd mustered.

Abby's mind raced to find an explanation. Pride insisted Daniel shouldn't guess what was really upsetting her.

"I haven't heard from Mrs. G.," she said quickly. Mrs. G. had told her she would be away until Friday, but Daniel didn't know that. "I guess I'm worried about what she's going to say."

A corner of Daniel's mouth lifted. "Has anyone else called you?"

"I have six appointments for estimates."

She didn't add that she had put them off for next week. Till after she had heard from Mrs. G. For some reason Abby felt Mrs. G.'s acceptance or refusal of her bid would be the star to set her future course by.

"Is that a copy of your bid?"

"Yes." She had been thinking of Daniel as she'd stared at the papers. Now Abby was glad she'd had them out. At least he hadn't caught her staring into space. That would be hard to explain.

"Would you mind if I took a look at it?"

"Of course not."

Abby watched Daniel skim the pages. The person she had come to know here was so different from the business expert who made his living giving seminars. Abby wondered if he regretted the time he'd spent here.

"This is excellently done."

Daniel looked at her curiously. Her color was high, accentuated by the warm pink shirt she wore.

"I'm just wondering if a ten-percent profit margin is too much. I'll order the drapes and the blinds through Veneers in the outlet plaza. The rest of the furniture and furnishings I'll find myself."

Daniel's eyes widened. "Too much? Too little is more like it. The ten-percent margin includes your time and labor. You've done a great job with the calculations, but you have to remember as your business builds you're going to have more overheads because you're going to be delegating more of the work."

She didn't want a huge company, just enough orders to enable her to do the work she loved.

"Besides, when you marry and start a family, you'll need more time for yourself."

Abby felt herself blush again. "I have no intention of getting married," she said.

An uncomfortable silence filled the office.

"Not ever?" Daniel made no effort to hide the surprise in his voice.

"N... not ever." Her report card had Failed scrawled in large red letters next to the subject of marriage.

Daniel looked at her for a minute and Abby thought he was going to say something. Instead he got to his feet. "Well, it's been a long day. Think I'll go for a run before I turn in. Want to come along?"

Abby thought of Daniel's muscles glistening with sweat. Her self-control didn't need stretching. "No, thanks," she said quickly. "I'll just finish what I'm working on."

Daniel wasn't a permanent part of her world. The loneliness the thought left in its wake frightened Abby. She didn't want anyone to have that kind of power over her again. Not ever.

As the door shut behind Daniel, Abby put her head down on her hands. Trying to make some kind of sense of her emotions seemed impossible. She didn't want Daniel to leave, yet she knew he couldn't stay. A thousand-piece puzzle would be easier to put together than the fragments of her muddled thoughts.

Mrs. G. called Abby early Friday evening and told her the job was hers.

"What made you select me?" Abby asked over the telephone. Shock made it hard for her to believe it was really true.

"Your prices are very reasonable and I liked the fact you didn't assume just because I had a big house I could afford the most expensive furnishings. Also, you aren't pushy, which is a big plus with me. I can see it's going to be fun working with you."

Abby felt as if she were floating on a cloud by the time she hung up. She had Daniel to thank for all this. He'd told her to be herself, and it had worked. If Mrs. G. liked her, chances were other people would too. Daniel had been right. Believing in one's abilities opened doors.

Abby had to find him and thank him right away. Rushing into the community room, she said, "Where's Daniel?"

Six pairs of eyes turned to look at her. Looks were exchanged. Knowing smiles appeared.

"He's gone out for a while," Sarah answered.

"I've got the job at Mrs. G.'s," announced Abby. "I can't believe it. This is going to help with the mortgage payment."

There was a small silence, and then Sarah said, "Abby, sit down for a minute, will you? There's something we've been wanting to talk to you about."

Abby slipped into a chair. "Yes, Gran?"

"You've done more than enough for us. I called Mr. Hawkins this morning and he's convinced the worst of our problems is behind us. Daniel is helping us with the catalog. Mail orders, plus keeping the store going will bring in more money than we'll need."

Abby noticed Gran wore her this-is-for-your-own-good look.

"We want you to keep all the profit you make from your interior-decorating business for yourself." Gran sounded very firm. "It was very generous of you to put your money into the store when we were going through the rough times, but we don't need your help financially anymore. It's time you started thinking of yourself."

"Life is short," Agnes added. "You have to stop worrying about us and concentrate on yourself."

"We are going to try and repay you as soon as possible," Gran said.

"The money doesn't matter," Abby said quickly.

"I know." Gran's smile was full of love as she looked at her. "It's just something we want to do over a period of time. We can never repay the amount of work and love you put in to save the store. I've hired Franz Koch and Jim Wong, so you'll be free now."

"Thanks, Gran."

Abby left the community room. Instead of feeling a load had slipped off her shoulders, she felt as if she had been cut adrift without an oar. Why had Gran been so firm about not needing her? Why the insistence she should get on with her own life?

Abby felt as if she'd arrived at a crossroads. She wasn't sure which direction to take now. Everything was changing so quickly. Daniel would be gone soon. The trio didn't need her anymore. She was free.

Free to do what? Abby wondered. Loneliness overwhelmed her as she looked at the papers on the desk in front of her. There was her work. She had to concentrate on that.

Mrs. G. had loved the idea of the master bedroom having lace curtains and a crocheted bedspread. It would be nice to be able to use some of the things from the store. Abby was glad she had set aside the things she'd thought she might need, before they'd been flooded with orders. The shop had looked bare this morning.

Deciding to go to the outlet plaza to see if she could find anything there for Mrs. G.'s house, Abby went out to the van. A change of scene might dispel this heaviness in her chest.

As she drove to the plaza, Abby told herself it was good that Gran had hired Franz and Jim. It would give her time to concentrate on Mrs. G.'s house. And of course, they hadn't cut her adrift. She would still spend her free time helping them.

In the plaza Abby found several furniture outlets. They promised her delivery in record time. Loaded down with catalogs, Abby looked for the fabric outlet she'd seen in the plaza map.

Gran and Agnes had implied life was a train and if one didn't get on at the right time, chances were one would be left stranded.

Abby squared her shoulders. She would work hard and make a success of her business. Her work would fill the gaps in her life.

She ran a hand through her hair. It didn't seem enough. There was a part of her that wanted more, that had been wanting more ever since Daniel Hawthorn had come into her life.

Abby's eyes widened as she stared blankly at the book of fabric samples. Her heart insisted there was more to life than simply her work. Courage wasn't easy to come by though. Maybe one day when her interior-decorating business was established, she would concentrate on her personal life.

To Abby, life seemed more like an obstacle race than a train. It had taken real effort to enter the race again by starting her own business. She wasn't sure she would be able to jump any other hurdles just yet.

"We'll be closing in fifteen minutes."

The announcement forced Abby to pay attention to the samples she had picked out. Surely she couldn't have spent an hour dreaming in the store?

Asking for swatches to be cut, she collected them and hurried out to the van. Her eyes narrowed as she got near it and saw the front left tire. It was flat.

A glance at her watch showed it was eight o'clock. The plaza was closing and the parking lot was almost deserted. She'd have to call Gran and tell her she needed a ride home. Tomorrow she'd get help changing the tire in the daylight.

"Don't worry about a thing," Gran assured her on the telephone. "Just wait by the main entrance to the plaza and someone will be there."

The car that pulled up ten minutes later was Daniel's.

"Hi!" Abby said breathlessly, as she opened the passenger door and slid into the seat. Looking at Daniel she said quickly, "I'm sorry you had to come get me. The van has a flat."

Her pounding heart made speech difficult as usual.

"I know. Not to worry." Daniel's voice was calm and re-assuring. "I'll change the tire in the morning. Have you locked the van?"

"Yes, though I don't know why anyone would want to steal it."

Abby wasn't aware she was staring at him till he smiled at her. "Is it so hard to imagine me changing a tire, Abby?"

"Of course not." She had been wondering if Daniel knew he had stolen her heart.

"I wasn't always an entrepreneur, you know. My first year in college, I worked part-time as a mechanic in a gas station."

It was hard to imagine Daniel with grease under his fin-gernails.

"Sarah tells me you've got the job with Mrs. G."

"Thanks to you," Abby said.

"No," Daniel corrected. "Thanks to *you*. You did this on your own, Abby. You had the flyers made and distributed, you wrote that bid."

"I wouldn't have been able to do it if you hadn't helped me look at life in a different way."

"Maybe I was a signpost of sorts," Daniel conceded, "but you chose to travel down the road. The credit for landing the job is all yours."

"I've told Mrs. G. I'll do one room first. If she likes it, I'll do the rest of her house."

Rome hadn't been built in one day. Abby felt it would take a lifetime of practice to get really confident.

"That sounds like a good idea."

To avoid any awkward pauses Abby told Daniel about some of her plans for the house. She put every bit of enthusiasm she could muster into her voice. He shouldn't guess how lost she was feeling. A little later, realizing he was very quiet, she lapsed into silence. Was Daniel bored by her chatter?

He had encouraged her to spread her wings, try to fly again. He should be happy she was so absorbed in her work. Daniel wondered why the emptiness had returned in full force.

She didn't see him as anything more than a friend. True, the steps from acquaintance to friend was progress. Without being quite sure what exactly he wanted, Daniel knew he wanted more than friendship with Abby. By encouraging Abby to this point he was running the risk of losing her.

How can you lose what you don't have in the first place, Hawthorn?

Abby's self-confidence needed the bolstering doing Mrs. G.'s house would give her. He was sure there would be more orders. He hadn't seen her so positive before. So happy. This was just what she needed.

He had to give her room to spread her wings.

Daniel didn't see Abby again till the next night at Hamish's class. She came in late. Right away he noticed her arms were full of books and that she looked tired but happy.

"How's it going?" He tried for casual.

"Great." There was a sparkle in her eyes as she took off her jacket and sat down. "How's the whittling going?"

Daniel glanced at the piece of wood in his hands. The more he worked on it, the less he liked it. Looking up he noticed the smile Abby tried to hide. "What do you think?"

"Well, it's kind of . . . different."

Trust Abby to find a way to make him feel good about the misshapen piece he was working on.

"I couldn't give it away if I tried," Daniel said gloomily.

"Oh, it's not so bad," said Abby quickly. "Gran always says, Beauty lies in the eyes of the beholder."

Daniel looked at Abby. Her hair gleamed and the silk scarf around her neck drew attention to the color in her face.

Abby saw Daniel's gaze fixed on her. She turned away quickly. Why hadn't he mentioned leaving yet?

A little later Abby stole a look at Daniel. She took in the strong hands, the curve of his well-shaped mouth with its sensuous lower lip. There was a frown between his brows as he concentrated on his whittling.

A shiver went through Abby. She didn't seem to be able to stop thinking of him, no matter what she did. Maybe staying away from him wasn't the right way to do things. Maybe proximity would strip her mind of these ridiculous longings. Proximity had destroyed what she had felt for Rod.

Determination surged like an enormous wave. Riding on the crest, Abby went up to Daniel after the class. "Going for a run tonight?"

"Yes," he said.

"If you wouldn't mind the company, I'll change and join you out front in five minutes with my bike."

What was Abby up to now? Her face wore the same look it had the day she had challenged him. The look people wore when they went into battle. Determined, daring, *apprehensive*. "Okay," he said quietly.

When she came out, Daniel noticed Abby was wearing walking shorts. It was a dark night and he couldn't see much of her, only her outline.

"Let's go." She hopped on the bike and started moving. The breathless note in her voice told him a great deal. She was flustered again.

"You should wear shorts more often," he said casually. "You have great legs."

Abby's bike wobbled. Daniel knew she'd chosen the shorts only because it was too dark for him or anyone else to see her properly.

"I don't look good in shorts."

The words confirmed his suspicion that Abby's lack of confidence extended to the way she looked. Right from the first time he'd seen her, Daniel had thought she was beautiful. But he knew low self-esteem was like a virus. It spread everywhere in one's system. It needed more than Agnes's brews to eradicate it.

"Have I ever told you I was called Totem Pole in high school?" Daniel said as Abby cycled slowly beside him. "I was all hands and legs, and my nose seemed bigger then than it does now."

"I was always big boned," confessed Abby, "and I hated it. Gran says I have my father's build."

His guess had been right. Abby's self-consciousness was the reason she hid herself in loose clothes.

"I think you're just the right size," said Daniel. "I've never been attracted to skinny women."

Abby almost fell off her bike. A double whammy. *You're just the right size. I've never been attracted to skinny women.*

Did Daniel mean he was attracted to *her?* She couldn't have heard right!

"Abby?"

"Yes?"

Daniel stopped and Abby put one foot on the ground for balance and turned to look at him. "I meant what I said. You're beautiful."

The words convinced Abby Daniel was working on his kindness again. "Th . . . thank you."

He surprised her by throwing one leg across the front wheel of her bicycle and gripping the handlebars. "Don't say thank you in that it's-nice-of-you-to-say-so-but-you-don't-have-to voice," he grated as Abby tried to steady herself, off balance in more ways than one.

"What do you want me to do?" she said, suddenly angry. "The fact that you've decided I'm beautiful doesn't change how I feel about myself."

The minute she said the words Abby wished them unspoken. Rod's displays of temper when she had answered him back had been awful.

"Will this?" Daniel asked, leaning toward her. One hand came up and held her shoulder while his mouth claimed hers. After a stunned moment, Abby put both arms around Daniel's neck.

The honking of a car horn forced them apart. Abby lowered her shaking hands to the handlebar of her cycle.

"I meant what I said." Huskiness had replaced Daniel's anger. "You are beautiful."

Reeling from the impact of the kiss, Abby merely nodded. For now she wanted to believe it.

Sarah looked at the others over the rim of her sewing glasses. "It wasn't easy telling Abby we didn't need her in the store anymore. Did you see the look on her face?"

"The shock will wear off," Agnes consoled. "We had to do what we did. Abby has to realize there's more to life than helping people."

"Daniel's a good man," Hamish said. "He told me today he's going to stay on and help us get the catalog ready."

"Maybe we should just leave them to it," Sarah reflected. "Maybe we are interfering too much. I mean, Abby's twenty-eight and Daniel's thirty-four. Surely they can get along without our help."

"It's what I've been saying from the start." Hamish opened his paper.

The two women looked at each other. Decision erased the doubt in their eyes.

"We have to do what we have to do," said Sarah.

Agnes nodded. "A nudge in time helps many a relationship."

Chapter Eight

From her window Abby watched Daniel come out of the guest house and look around him. "Princess, come here."

The German shepherd took one look at him, gave a small "woof" and chased Muffy into the woods behind the house.

Abby hoped Daniel realized Princess would never be the same again. She closed her eyes. *She* would never be the same again. Lying awake last night reliving Daniel's kiss, she'd realized proximity hadn't improved anything.

She stared at the trees remembering how bare they had been the day Daniel had come to Carbon Canyon. Now they were covered with shiny new leaves and fat buds. The magnolia Gramps had planted when she was born was in full bloom. Hope and the promise of spring was everywhere. If only she could absorb some of it.

She hoped work would block out thoughts of Daniel. Mrs. G. had selected the samples she liked best from the swatches Abby had taken to her. The next step was to order the drapes from Veneers.

Abby wondered where the books she'd picked up from the library the day before were. There was a design in one of them she wanted made up for Mrs. G.'s living room.

The last time she'd seen them had been in the community room. She'd have to go get them before she could proceed with her work.

As soon as he saw Abby leave the house, Daniel got to his feet and headed for the community room. The living-room window of the guest house faced the front door of Sarah's house. Seated at the desk by the window, his vigil hadn't allowed him to concentrate on mapping out his new book, but it had paid off.

Abby picked up her books and turned to leave when she heard Daniel say behind her, "There you are, Abby. Would you like to go for a drive with me?"

Immediately a silence fell in the community room, and Abby felt everyone look at her. She stared at Daniel. What was wrong with him? Why had he blurted out his invitation in front of twenty people?

"It won't take long," he coaxed. "You need a break from work."

"All right." She had to get away from the curious looks.

"This won't take long," Daniel repeated as they headed for his car.

Abby recalled the first time Daniel had told her he wanted to show her something. It had been the night of the play. She had been terrified. Now she glanced at his profile. Trust had replaced that earlier uneasiness around him. Fear was not a word she could ever associate with Daniel.

Daniel followed Carbon Canyon Road and pulled up in front of a house tucked halfway up the hillside. A For Sale sign hung in the front yard. Getting out of the car Abby noticed the house was set on a couple of acres of land. The redwood-and-glass exterior made it blend in beautifully with the massive pine trees that surrounded it.

"It's beautiful," Abby said.

"Want to look inside?" Daniel asked, pleased with her reaction.

"Do you have a key?"

He held up a set. "Picked it up from the Realtors this morning."

For Daniel to have a key to the place, he must be a serious potential buyer. Abby stared at the house blankly as she walked up the path to the massive double doors.

If Daniel bought a house in Carbon Canyon that would complicate everything. She could hold out against him for a little while, but running into him on a daily or weekly basis was going to complicate her life.

Besides, what did Daniel want with the house? A house went hand in hand with marriage and children. Settling down. Abby didn't want to see Daniel with a wife and child.

Her churning thoughts produced a layer of uneasiness in Abby's mind.

Daniel unlocked the door and stood aside to let Abby enter. Her first impression was of light and space. As they walked through the rooms, Daniel said, "An architect designed this for an actor who planned on living here. It was barely finished before the man changed his mind and decided to sell it. That's why the carpeting isn't in yet and the walls haven't been painted."

Abby didn't blame the actor. Rod had hated coming here even for the weekends, calling it a hick town for old fogeys. "Living in Carbon Canyon is different from visiting it. Don't rush into a decision to buy the house."

"Are you saying I might get tired of Carbon Canyon?" Daniel asked. "I don't think I will. Being here these last few weeks has made me realize I want to put down roots. I'm tired of being a rolling stone."

Their gazes meshed and Abby had a hard time looking away. "What about your work?"

"I intend to cut down on my seminars, and I can write my books here just as well as I can anywhere else. Besides, L.A. is only an hour away."

Abby's gaze skittered away from Daniel's. "And your business?"

"After my accident I appointed an executive director to run the company."

It was like a game of volleyball. She had no right to toss questions at him. The fact Daniel was tossing answers back at her without any hesitation told her how serious he was about his plans.

"This is a beautiful house," she said awkwardly as they went through the place.

It had five bedrooms and a huge bonus room on the second floor. Outside there was an enormous deck and a huge backyard.

"Princess will love the extra space."

Abby wondered if Daniel was planning a large family.

"I think I'll have to get another dog when I move here. Princess is going to miss Muffy badly."

Daniel sounded deadly serious about buying the house and moving to Carbon Canyon. She would have to find a way of dealing with it.

His next words took her breath away. "Will you help me choose the carpeting and furnish the house, Abby, when you're done with Mrs. G.'s?"

"Of course." Abby ran a hand through her hair. She owed Daniel that much at least for all his help.

"There's something about this house." Daniel's voice sounded reflective. "As soon as I stepped into it, I got the feeling it was the one for me."

He was right. Abby could picture the house filled with flowers and children and pets. It was a house for living and loving.

He could tell she liked the house. What Daniel wanted to know was how Abby felt about him. Intuition hinted this might be a good time for the questions he wanted answered. Caution disagreed.

Daniel saw the glow in Abby's eyes and decided to take a risk.

"Abby, have you ever wanted a place of your own?" Something about the way her expression changed made Daniel add quickly, "I'm not implying you shouldn't be living with Sarah or anything like that, I just wondered . . ." He stopped himself before he said anything to complicate matters.

"I know what you mean," Abby said. "I've thought of living on my own, but I can't afford it right now."

"Would Sarah be very hurt if you moved out?"

Sarah didn't seem possessive about Abby, but one never knew.

Abby looked surprised. "Gran's the most independent person I know. She's always said she wouldn't mind where I was as long as she knew I was happy."

"I see."

Opening the patio door she stepped out. Daniel followed.

"Have you made an offer on the house?" Abby asked. It was time to change the subject. She didn't want any more help rearranging her life just yet.

Seeing this house, realizing Daniel intended to stay on in Carbon Canyon, unsettled her.

"Not yet." Daniel locked the front door and checked it. "I wasn't one-hundred-percent sure I wanted it till... till... now."

Abby, busy admiring the landscaping, didn't notice Daniel's hesitation on the last two words.

"Houses give out vibes just as people do," she said without thinking.

"They do?" Daniel stopped on the path and stared at her in surprise. "What kind of vibrations is this house giving out?"

"I sense a great yearning. It's waiting to be filled with happiness and a family."

The little silence that followed her statement made Abby say nervously, "I know it sounds silly, but that's how I feel. Mrs. G.'s house will always be elegant and a showpiece, but somehow I can't see a family there."

Daniel remained silent. A part of him hoped what Abby said was true. That this house and the person who shared it with him would dispel the last vestiges of his own emptiness. More and more he wanted Abby to be that person.

She might not admit it, but Daniel was sure she felt the way he did. There was fire in her kisses, hunger in her response. He didn't expect commitment of any kind. Not at first. All he wanted to know was that Abby was as eager to explore what was between them as he was.

Getting Abby to acknowledge there might be something between them would be the first step. It was also the hardest one.

Two days later Abby stepped off the bus from L.A. at eight o'clock at night. She'd spent most of the day ordering furniture for Mrs. G.'s house. The delivery date, ten days away, ensured there was enough time for the wallpapering and the painting to be done. Hiring three of Gran's friends for that part of the job had been a good idea.

Busy with her thoughts, Abby didn't see Daniel till he came right up to her. "Hi!"

The happiness that filled Abby at the sight of Daniel turned her brain to mush. "What are you doing here?"

"Sarah mentioned you'd be on this bus. I thought I'd give you a ride home. Let me take that."

Daniel reached for the large package she'd been carrying. Reluctantly Abby handed it over.

"It's glass," she cautioned.

"I'll make sure it's safe," Daniel assured her, placing it on the back seat of his car.

They were on their way home when Abby said, "I could have walked. It isn't so far."

"I could have taken you into L.A. if you'd told me you were going," countered Daniel.

"I always go to L.A. by bus. The van's too old for these trips."

Maybe next year this time, if things continued to go well, she'd be able to buy a less decrepit set of wheels. The year after, she might rent a place of her own.

The thought of Abby carrying that heavy package and waiting for the bus bothered Daniel. "Why is it so difficult for you to ask for anything for yourself, Abby?"

"I don't know what you mean."

She did. One man had robbed her of her independence, and ever since she had guarded it carefully.

"Would it have been so hard to ask me for a ride into L.A.?" The more he thought about it, the angrier Daniel got.

It wasn't asking for the ride that would have been difficult. The thought of being with Daniel for so long was scary. Abby wasn't sure she wouldn't say or do something that would reveal how she felt around him. Unsure, excited, *stormy*.

"Sometimes by asking for help, you give another person a chance to feel good about giving as well," Daniel said quietly.

"I prefer not to be under any kind of obligation to anyone," Abby said stiffly.

"Why? Are you afraid I might expect something in return?"

"No. Gran and Gramps just taught me to be self-reliant." That wasn't it. She was afraid to trust. Afraid of being hurt again.

The city lights below them made Daniel realize he had taken Carbon Canyon Road, instead of turning to Sarah's house. Daniel stopped the car at the same spot they'd come to after the play. Maybe this was a good time to say what was on his mind.

"Do you think it's easy for me to accept free board and lodge, even have my laundry done for me? I'm glad I stayed, though it went against the grain. Being here has done wonders for me. My neurologist thinks the improvement in my hands is due in part to the fact that I'm under no stress at all now."

A part of Abby knew Daniel would insist on a reply to his original question. For now there was something else she had to know.

"Were you stressed when you came to Carbon Canyon?" she asked Daniel. Her first impression of him h~~~ been of someone perfectly in control of his life.

"Stress isn't always the visible kind," ~~~ "Sometimes though a person appe~~~ stress can manifest itself as an illness, ~~~ lay recovery."

"You seemed so sure of yourself at the seminar...." Abby's voice trailed away. She didn't want Daniel to remember how she had challenged him.

"I was more or less playing a part. The part of the perfect speaker. I had even begun to think there was nothing more to life than work and success. It took these weeks here to show me how wrong I was."

"What caused the accident?" Watching Daniel's mouth tighten, Abby wished the words unsaid.

"You don't have to talk about it, if you don't want to," she said quickly.

Daniel looked up. Confusion pooled in Abby's face. "I don't mind talking about it, now." Clearing his throat, he continued, "My fiancée and I were going home from a party. We were having an argument. The car crashed into the hillside. Eve died on the spot."

There was so much he'd left out. So much he couldn't bring himself to explain.

The geyser of pain that shot up inside Abby at Daniel's words flooded her throat. It was hard to say anything, but she managed to get the words out. "It wasn't your fault."

Daniel looked at her as if she'd taken leave of her senses. "What do you mean?"

"The accident," said Abby. "No matter what you think, it wasn't your fault."

"How can you say that?" Daniel demanded. "You weren't there."

"I know you."

Daniel waited for the rest. Only silence followed.

I know you.

The simple, direct way Abby said the words, the conviction in her voice, filled him with warmth.

Abby sat in silence watching Daniel's face. Deep within she knew he blamed himself for the accident.

"I could have been drunk," Daniel pointed out.

"Except that you don't drink," Abby said. "Hamish always offers you an after-dinner brandy, and you refuse."

"I could have been driving rashly."

"You are too responsible a person to do anything rash."

Abby's faith in him stripped away the silence he had shrouded the past in.

"Eve was angry with me that evening," Daniel said slowly. "Though we'd been living together for a year, our relationship had deteriorated. She broke off our engagement on the way to the party. I told her that was fine with me. We had less in common than we'd thought."

Daniel stared straight ahead. He shouldn't have started this. Opening up this part of himself was very difficult.

"At the party Eve drank heavily and started flirting with a stranger there. She told me she wanted to leave the party with him. I really had no right to do so, but I insisted she come home with me. I couldn't let her go in that state. On the way home, she started arguing again, accused me of being cold and domineering. When I wouldn't say anything, she grabbed the wheel. The car spun out of control and we crashed into a pole. Eve died on the spot."

"It wasn't your fault."

Abby made a great cheerleader, but Daniel still had something else to say. "If I had let her leave the party with that other man, she wouldn't have died that night."

"You acted in her best interest," Abby said quietly. "That's all we can do when we care about someone."

"I did care for Eve," Daniel acknowledged softly, " I didn't love her."

He wasn't sure he could define love.

Daniel glanced at Abby as he reversed the car and headed back. He'd never felt this urge to spend every free minute with anyone else. He admired Abby's courage and her ability to help others, even her independence.

No one else had ever set his heart pounding with a look. Her kisses drove him crazy. The desire to take care of her wouldn't go away.

Did all these symptoms add up to love? And, if it did, would he ever get a chance to tell Abby so?

"Thank you for the ride, Daniel."

Abby stepped out of the car quickly when it stopped beside the guest house. She didn't want to tangle with him while he was in this mood. The tension in the car had been thick. It was easier to run than stay and talk things over.

Later in her room, Abby unwrapped the package and stared at the ceiling lamp she had bought. It would be perfect for the breakfast nook in Daniel's new house. Abby ran a hand through her hair. How was she going to explain why she had bought the lamp to Daniel?

Tired but restless, Abby decided to go outside for a while. She hadn't seen the dogs all day. Maybe spending a little time with them would help her relax and fall asleep quickly.

She hoped Daniel would forget the little argument they'd had earlier. But then it really hadn't been an argument. How could it, when one person refused to stand and fight? The thought that running had become a habit she couldn't control nagged at Abby from time to time.

Chapter Nine

Daniel put his hand into the back pocket of his jogging shorts and brought it out empty. He frowned. What had he done with the key to the guest house?

He retraced the evening. After dinner he had brushed Princess' coat, then played with her and Muffy for a while. Later he had watched the news on television. He'd left a message on the realty firm's answering machine, saying he would be in the office first thing in the morning to make an offer on the house. As he'd changed and left for his run he'd been thinking of the way Abby had looked in the house. So exactly right. For the house. For *him*.

Since their talk yesterday, the compulsion to tell her how he felt about her was mounting. Daniel frowned. Had he forgotten to take his key along?

Hoping he'd left his bedroom window open, Daniel went around the side of the guest house and tried it, but it was firmly shut. He turned toward the main house, glancing at his watch. It was just after eight. He hated disturbing anyone at this hour, but he had no other choice.

"Hello, Daniel," Sarah said opening the front door. "Come in. You're just in time for a cup of coffee and a piece of pie."

"I can't stay," he told her quickly. "I just wondered if I could have a spare key to the guest house. I seem to have locked myself out."

"Come in for a minute, while I ask Hamish for it," Sarah repeated.

"We don't have a spare key," Hamish reminded Sarah, in answer to her question. "Franz lost it when he painted the guest house for us and I haven't had another made. You'll have to sleep here tonight, Daniel. We'll get a locksmith out, tomorrow."

Ten minutes later Daniel found himself standing under the shower. He was to sleep in Sarah's family room for tonight. They had produced a clean pair of his pajamas from the pile of laundry they insisted on doing for him. His objections had been bulldozed the minute they left his mouth. It had been easier to give in.

When Daniel disappeared into the bathroom, Sarah said, "Oh, dear, I forgot to tell him we do have a key for the door that leads into the guest house from the community room."

There wasn't a single trace of repentance on her face. In fact she looked absolutely content with her loss of memory.

"I forgot, too," Agnes chimed in happily. "After all, what can you expect of us at our age?"

They exchanged smiles filled with mischief before turning to Hamish.

"What about you Hamish?" Sarah asked. "You never forget anything."

Hamish picked up his newspaper. Sometimes it was the only defence he had against the women.

"I, er, well, it just slipped my mind," he mumbled from behind it.

After his shower Daniel picked up his clothes and shoes and padded to the living room. The sleeper had been pulled out and made up. Deciding to turn in, Daniel wondered where Abby was. No one had mentioned her, and he hadn't asked, though he wanted to know very badly.

His eyes narrowed at the sight of the glass of milk on the side table beside the queen-size sleeper. His mother had always insisted he drink a big glass of milk at night. He could picture her so clearly. Warm, laughing, happy. His father had been his best friend. Always ready to listen, to explain things to him.

For the first time ever, his memories flooded him with warmth, only warmth. He experienced none of the pain or bitterness that usually accompanied the thoughts of his parents. They hadn't abandoned him. Death had cheated them just as it had cheated him, but nothing could kill the good memories of the time they had spent together. Strange that it had taken him all these years to see that part of his life in its proper perspective. Being here, knowing Abby, had changed him in so many ways.

Switching off the light, Daniel slipped into bed. He wasn't ashamed of the wetness on his cheeks. It was the first time he had cried for his parents, without being angry with them. Understanding took the pain of bitterness out of his grief.

It was midnight before Abby looked at the clock on the nightstand. Her neck ached from bending over her work, but she felt good about all she had accomplished. Totaling all her purchases had shown her she was well within Mrs.

G.'s budget. At this rate, she might be able to buy that hall table and the mirror she had seen at the outlet plaza for the enormous entryway. It would look spectacular with a huge urn filled with dried, painted fronds beside it.

Abby put a hand up to her mouth as she yawned. A glass of milk would help relax her keyed-up mind. Getting to her feet, she went to the door.

The first thump woke Daniel. Opening his eyes he realized he was in Sarah Trenton's living room. The scent of rose petals drifted to his nostrils from the sheets. Everything was silent now, but he was sure he hadn't imagined the thump. A wedge of light flowed into the living room. Daniel turned over on his front. Under his fingers, the cool cotton pillowcase felt comfortably soft. Another thump had him on his feet. He had to investigate the sound. Daniel followed the light into the kitchen.

Abby was bent over, reaching for something inside the refrigerator. Daniel barely noticed the two cans on the shiny kitchen floor. His gaze was held by a shapely behind clad in something Christmas-green and satiny. Below, a pair of legs went on forever.

Daniel coughed. Under the circumstances, it seemed the gentlemanly sort of thing to do.

Abby whirled, clutching a loaf of bread to her chest.

"What are you doing here?" she gasped.

"I locked myself out of the guest house. The trio invited me to sleep here tonight."

His gaze seemed stuck to the neckline of the two-piece garment Abby wore. It plunged into a V, revealing a satisfying expanse of creamy skin. His hands itched to reach out and brush aside the two thin straps that held the garment up. He wished the loaf of bread wouldn't obstruct his view.

Aware of the way his heart was pounding, Daniel said nothing, merely continued to look at Abby.

"No one is ever up at this hour." Abby edged sideways till she was behind the kitchen table.

"A noise in here woke me."

"I'm sorry. I was reaching for the milk. I didn't realize somebody had filled the refrigerator with these cans till they all started falling out. I think I'll go to bed now."

Daniel watched the way she eyed the door out of the kitchen. Moving away from it, he said, "Let me get the milk out for you."

When he placed it on the table, he saw Abby had exchanged the loaf of bread for a tray. She held it to her chest as if it were a shield.

"Don't," said Daniel, pouring milk into a mug.

"Don't what?" he heard Abby ask defensively.

"Don't feel embarrassed. You look beautiful in that."

"It's a birthday present from Gran." Abby spoke in a rush, as if to let him know she would never have bought a garment like this herself.

"Sarah has the best taste in the world." Daniel reached for the tray and took it out of Abby's unresisting hands.

Placing his hand on the curve of her neck, he massaged her collarbone with his thumb. Abby stared at him, hypnotized.

"Don't," she said stiffly.

"Why not?" asked Daniel. "Don't you like it?"

Like it? Abby felt as if only her skin held her jangled system together. Inside, everything had shattered into a million shards of excitement.

Daniel's forefinger traced the neckline of Abby's nightwear. Lightly, casually, *lovingly*. A muffled groan escaped Abby as his eyes followed the route his finger took. His head came up at the sound and Abby saw the reflection of her own heightened tension in his eyes.

She swayed forward, as he leaned towards her.

"Ahem!" said Agnes from the doorway.

They both sprang apart and turned. Guilt bounced off their faces, making them look like little children.

"I need some water to take a sleeping pill." Agnes opened a cabinet and took out a glass. "I see you can't sleep, either."

"I came down for some milk," Abby said quickly.

"I heard a noise and got up to investigate," Daniel added.

Agnes filled a glass with water and turned to stare at them over the rim.

"Good night." Abby turned and fled without the milk she had come for.

Daniel made a hasty retreat to the living room and sat on the edge of his bed.

Neither of them heard Agnes chuckle as she went back to her room. She couldn't wait to tell Sarah what she'd just witnessed. Not mentioning the other key had worked wonders.

Abby looked out of the window of her room as she ran a shaking hand through her hair. Picking up a pillow she hugged it to her chest. Blood pounded through her entire body.

You're beautiful.

No one had made her believe in the words before. Not in the way Daniel did. The intensity in his eyes had burned into her brain, rendering her powerless to think.

Daniel lay down and stared at the ceiling. Had he gone mad? If Agnes hadn't arrived when she had, he would have picked Abby up and carried her off to bed. The thought of her in his arms, her green eyes hazed with passion, made Daniel groan.

He hadn't meant to scare her. Knowing Abby, what had happened tonight would be enough for her to put on a repeat performance of her turtle act. Pull back into the shell she had constructed for herself. He had to get to her before she did that.

He had to talk to her, tell her about the effect she was having on him. He would go crazy if he didn't.

Abby was surprised to see Daniel by her van when she came out the next morning. Princess and Muffy were with him. To all intents and purposes, he was throwing old tennis balls for the dogs to fetch. Instinct told Abby he was waiting for her. Her mouth went dry.

"Abby," Daniel said as she paused on the step. Being reminded of the way he'd looked at her last night made a pulse throb in Abby's throat.

"I want to talk to you."

His voice gave nothing away but suddenly Abby remembered how his hand had felt against her skin. Heat flooded her. Pulling her jacket tighter around her she said, "What about?"

After a pause, he said, "Would you like to go to a jazz concert with me Saturday night?"

The only other time she'd heard Daniel hesitate was when he'd come into The Busy Bee for the first time.

"I can't, Saturday night," Abby said. "It's Nan Harper's anniversary and I agreed to stay with her father, while she and her husband go out for dinner and a movie."

And if it hadn't been sitting with Fred Harper, it would have been something else. Impatience surged through him. Daniel could recite the list by heart. Taking someone's dog to the vet, giving a haircut, reading to someone or simply keeping a bedside vigil.

Daniel took a deep breath, let it out slowly. It didn't cool his temper any. "When are you going to stop hiding behind all these people you help, Abby?"

Abby felt the color rise in her face. "I'm not hiding behind anyone."

"Yes, you are. You're scared to come out with me. Going back to the work you love doing has been a small step up, but you've still got your personal feelings locked away in cold storage."

Why had she ever thought Daniel Hawthorn was kind and understanding?

"If my feelings are in cold storage, they're there for a good reason." Abby was furious. She only hoped Daniel wouldn't mistake the tears of rage in her eyes for anything else. "No one has the right to tell me when I should bring them out, least of all you. You're here to help The Busy Bee, not me. You might want to keep that in mind."

Halfway to Mrs. G.'s house, Abby's anger began to fade. Fairness insisted she was just upset because Daniel was right. She had locked her feelings away and hidden behind people to avoid him in the beginning. But not this time. If Nan hadn't asked her to sit with Fred, she would have loved to go to the concert with Daniel.

Abby ran a hand through her hair. The man was impossible.

You went and blew it, Hawthorn. Blew it sky-high.

Daniel wished he hadn't been so rough with Abby. He had sounded like a class-one jerk. Maybe he should take her advice and concentrate on the store. As Abby had pointed out, that was why he was here in the first place.

The flowers were delivered in the middle of the morning. Daniel answered the knock on the door of the office with an absentminded, "Yes?"

The door opened, but no one said anything. He looked up. Sarah and Agnes stood there, beaming smiles on their faces.

"For you." Sarah held the flowers out.

"A boy brought them just now," Agnes added.

Daniel's eyes widened. No one had ever sent him flowers. Six perfect orange rosebuds nestled in a bed of jungle-green fern.

"There's a card with them," Sarah pointed out, placing them on the table.

"We'll get back to our work." Agnes's voice was filled with reluctance.

"No, stay." Taking the card, he opened it.

I'm free Saturday after next. The message was in Abby's handwriting. Daniel's mouth went dry.

"They're from Abby," he said, reading the message over and over again.

More important than agreeing to go out with him was the fact she had made this move on her own. Abby was reaching out to him.

He lifted his gaze to the doorway. There was no one there. Picking up the telephone he called Ticketron for reservations to the concert. Daniel kept looking at the flowers as he ordered his tickets, unable to believe Abby had really sent them.

Whoever took on Abby had to realize he would have to share her with the rest of the world. Abby was a giver. She would always be one.

Who are you trying to kid, Hawthorn? Cut the whoever bit, and admit you see yourself in that role.

Since college he'd always had a plan. Having plans had shielded him from disappointment. From defeat. Now he had come up against something that couldn't be planned. Love.

He had to take each day as it came and hope things would work out for the best. Right now, hope seemed a very insecure hook on which to hang the future.

Daniel's thoughts paced the floor of his mind. There had to be something he could do. He hadn't felt as frustrated and powerless as this in a long while. Since his parents' death in fact. Maybe that was why he had chosen a career in business. He knew exactly what reaction a certain action would produce.

Human relations weren't like that at all. There was no order to them, at times no sense. Yet, nobody who wanted to live a completely satisfying life could avoid the tangle of relationships. Pain was part of the package, just as pleasure was.

At their next meeting, the trio took turns thanking Daniel.

"We're going to learn by all the advice you've given us," said Hamish. "Each month we're going to make sure we have the mortgage payment before we give anything except our time away."

Agnes nodded solemnly. "Franz has enrolled in a computer class in adult education, and as soon as we can afford it, we're going to buy a computer."

"You've decided not to accept the oil company's offer to sponsor you?" Daniel had guessed they wouldn't take that way out.

"We voted on it," Sarah said, "and though the offer would have meant we'd be financially secure for the rest of our lives, none of us wants to be taken over. We want to continue the way we are, make our own rules. No corporation can understand us better than we can understand ourselves."

It felt good to see them so happy. He hadn't done much but the results were wonderful. None of his other business accomplishments had given him this warm feeling inside.

Nothing beat this, except having Abby in his arms. He looked at her. She'd chosen the chair next to his, and her scent had interfered with his concentration throughout the last half hour. Saturday night was only two days away.

"How's it going?"

"Tomorrow we start wallpapering and painting," Abby told him. "Mrs. G.'s housewarming date doesn't give me a whole lot of time, but I know I can do it."

"I guess I'll see you Saturday." He had to be patient till then. It was obvious she had her hands full right now.

"Saturday," Abby echoed with a quick smile. "I'm looking forward to the concert."

Chapter Ten

Abby was in Mrs. G.'s house Saturday morning when she started sneezing. It had been so long since her allergies had bothered her that she ignored the attack at first. Anything could be causing it. The paint thinner the workmen were using, the paint itself. It would just go away.

A half hour later Abby's eyes were watering so badly she couldn't keep them open. Telling the workers she'd be back soon, she went outside. A breath of fresh air would take care of everything.

When she couldn't stop sneezing, Abby decided to go home. It was time to follow her doctor's advice. A change of surroundings and an antihistamine would soon set everything straight.

Abby wasn't sure if the pounding was inside her head, or outside. Opening her eyes was an effort. Someone was at the front door. Reaching for her robe, she went groggily downstairs.

Abby clung to the front door. Was she dreaming? Daniel stood there in a dark suit, looking like he had when she'd first seen him.

"You aren't ready?"

Abby looked down. The bunny feet on her yellow flannel pajamas peeped out from under her robe. She remembered putting them on because she'd felt cold.

"Ready?" she said blankly, wishing the antihistamine didn't always make her head feel so heavy.

"The concert," Daniel reminded patiently.

"Oh my goodness!" Abby ran a hand through her hair. "I've been asleep. Why didn't someone wake me?" Turning away from the door, she went through the hall into the kitchen. "Where is everyone, anyway?"

No one had woken her because she hadn't told anyone about the concert. She'd thought it was better not to mention it.

"It's bingo night," Daniel reminded her.

"I wasn't feeling well and I took an antihistamine—" Abby's voice was threaded with nervousness "—but I'll be ready in five minutes."

She had planned for this evening, wanted everything to be perfect. Daniel must be very angry with her.

Abby turned away quickly. It was a mistake. Her head spun and she felt the room whirl around her. Grabbing the back of a chair, she hung on.

"Abby, what's wrong?"

"Antihistamines have this effect on me."

"Sit down." Daniel put her into a chair. Bringing her a glass of water he said, "Should we go to a doctor?"

"No," Abby said quickly. "I'll be fine."

She had been meaning to ask Dr. Davisson for a different prescription, but as usual she hadn't found time for her personal needs.

The feeling she had ruined the evening clung to her. "I'm sorry. I was perfectly fine this morning. Something at Mrs. G.'s triggered my allergies." Looking at the kitchen clock, Abby said, "You can still make it to the concert if you leave now." There was no sense in both of them missing it.

"I'm not going without you. I'll be right back."

Abby gathered her robe around her. If she closed her eyes she could see a mirror image of what she must look like. Yellow flannel pajamas with bunny feet. Old blue robe. Hair standing up. Sleep-drenched face.

A surge of adrenaline got her to her feet. Abby headed for the downstairs bathroom. After washing her face and brushing her teeth, she combed her hair, using water to control its unruliness. It didn't help much, but it was a slight improvement.

"In here," Daniel called as she opened the door of the bathroom.

Abby came to a dead stop in the doorway of the family room. Daniel had moved the coffee table aside and was spreading a picnic blanket over the carpet.

"What are you doing?"

"This is the next best thing to going to the concert," he said.

Dazed, Abby sat down. She recognized the distinctive basket. It was from the Roebuck deli on Main Street. The place had a reputation for elegance and style.

Daniel had gone to a great deal of trouble arranging the evening.

"I'm sorry." Abby took the exquisite china plate Daniel handed her. She should never have taken the antihistamine.

"Don't be," Daniel said, picking up his own plate and leaning against the sofa. "Staying in is all the style these days."

"It is?" Abby asked blankly.

"Yes. People have such busy life-styles with business lunches and hectic schedules, spending an evening at home has become special. It's the latest thing in Los Angeles, anyway."

The white wine Daniel had poured into crystal goblets was perfect with the chicken cordon bleu. Daniel looked elegant in his formal clothes. He didn't seem upset to be sitting on the floor in them. Abby glanced down at her outfit. Talk about an odd note. She didn't fit in here. The thought turned the food in her mouth to sawdust. Daniel deserved better than this.

"Relax, Abby."

She stared at Daniel as he got up and slipped a tape into the VCR. How did he always guess what she was thinking?

Daniel knew she was upset about how things had turned out. Abby had watched him as if she expected him to explode any minute. Another ex-husband speciality, Daniel guessed. The best thing to do was ignore it.

Switching off the overhead light, he left the room bathed in the golden glow of a single lamp. Sitting next to Abby so that they were both resting against the couch, he said, "This is the next best thing to being there. I bought this tape of the International Jazz Festival for you, but we may as well listen to it together now."

Daniel had bought the tape for her?

As Abby lost herself in the beauty of the music, her mood shifted. Her clothes, her hair, nothing seemed to matter anymore. It felt right to be here, beside Daniel, listening to some of the best music in the world.

She wasn't quite sure when he picked up the afghan from the back of the couch. Moving closer to her, he placed it around both their shoulders. Abby enjoyed the feeling of being tucked into his side, the heat emanating from him.

"Have you ever been to New Orleans?" Daniel asked.

"No."

"We'll go there one day and you can have your fill of jazz. It's performed everywhere. The streets, the sidewalk cafés, the best hotels."

Abby wondered if she'd heard right. Had Daniel said *we?* Her glance went to the screen. Fireworks signaled the end of the concert. They seemed to be some going off inside her as well.

Sensing Daniel watching her, Abby looked at him, and everything else faded away. The room, the television screen, the remains of their picnic. Emotion throbbed between them, and her heart beat to the strange rhythm of magic drums.

Daniel leaned forward and took her face in his hands. Abby's hands went around his neck. His lips were warm and wine-fresh against hers. She opened her mouth, welcoming his heat. His love.

She had been out in the cold for so long. It felt good to be warm again. To feel as if she'd come home.

Every nerve ending responded to Daniel's touch. Abby cuddled closer, enjoying the feel of the powerful muscles in his back under her hands.

Daniel loved having Abby in his arms. He kissed her brows, her cheeks, the tip of her nose before returning to her mouth for more. It was a while before his lips wandered down her neck and he pushed aside her dressing gown and her pajamas, resting his mouth against a bare shoulder.

"Daniel, no."

He went very still and then he lifted his head. "Abby, what's the matter?"

The passion she saw on Daniel's face made Abby very nervous. "I—I want you to leave now."

"Abby," he made to draw her close again, but she put a hand on his chest.

"Daniel, wait, please. This is all happening too fast for me."

She brought her other hand up, increasing the distance between them. She'd followed emotion in a headlong flight once before. Never again. She couldn't let Daniel sweep her off her feet. The magic of his kiss was all part of the illusion he had created tonight. The picnic in the family room, the wine, the wonderful concert. What they felt now wouldn't stand up to the light of day, tomorrow.

"Abby, what's wrong?"

She let her hands drop. "Daniel, please don't rush me."

"I don't think I am rushing you. If I go any slower, I won't be moving at all. Why deny what we both feel?"

"Because it's happening too fast," said Abby. "Because it's happened before, and I can't trust these feelings again."

"I'm not a clone of your late husband, Abby."

"It's not you I don't trust," she said quickly. "It's myself. I'm not ready for any of this."

She hadn't forgotten how quickly she had fallen out of love with Rod.

They looked at each other in silence. For a minute she thought Daniel was about to argue with her.

"I'm sorry." She'd never seen him look so tense, not even when she'd challenged him at the seminar.

"It's all right, Abby."

Long after the front door closed behind him, Abby sat gazing at the blank television screen. Daniel's quiet words haunted her. *It's all right, Abby.*

Only it wasn't all right.

Memory played the blues as she repacked the picnic basket. The feeling she'd lost something very important clung to her as she went upstairs.

Abby thought of Daniel's words the next evening as she parked in the drive of his new house and stared at it. It looked better than the first time, because the rays of the setting sun had polished the house to a soft amber.

Carefully taking out the lamp, Abby extracted the key to the house from her pocket. It had been an impulse to come here today.

She had gone to Irving Realtors this morning. Marge Irving, who ran the real-estate company with her husband, had gone to school with Abby. Getting the key had been no problem. Marge had told her Daniel's offer on the property had been accepted. She had also mentioned that as he was a pre-qualified buyer, escrow would go through very quickly.

Going into the kitchen, Abby hung the lamp on the hook suspended from the ceiling fixture. Glancing out of the window she stared at the row of trees. They looked as if they had been there forever. Why couldn't love be like that?

Abby touched her mouth. The imprint of Daniel's lips was still strong on hers. She closed her eyes. Daniel had made a ceremony out of the kiss. It had all been there out in the open. In the way she had kissed him. In the way she had held him. She wanted Daniel.

She had a poor way of showing it, though. Fear had made her push him away blindly. There had been anger mixed in with his tension. Abby didn't blame him. She felt angry with herself, too.

They had known each other for over a month now. Seen each other practically every day. Spent time together. That could hardly be called rushing someone.

She'd done what she'd become expert at. Run from the situation.

"Hi, Abby!"

She whirled to face Daniel, her heart in her throat.

"You scared me."

He looked very handsome in a yellow T-shirt and brown slacks, his wet hair slicked back. Abby's gaze wandered to the width of his shoulders. Imagination replayed the way his back, bunched with tension, had felt under her hands. Molten heat flooded her. Abby swallowed.

"I'm sorry," Daniel said. "I saw your van outside. I called out but you didn't answer."

Abby flushed. Her thoughts had blanketed her senses. "I didn't hear you."

His gaze went from her to the lamp.

"A small present from all of us to thank you for your help," Abby said quickly. Including the trio in the gift provided good cover. "I hope you don't mind me coming here like this."

"Of course not."

"If you don't like it, I can take it back." Daniel might not want an imitation-Tiffany lamp when he could afford the real thing.

"I like it." Something about the way Daniel looked at her made Abby uneasy. "You're the expert. I'm looking forward to your help doing up the place. Will you have the time?"

He still wanted her to help? She couldn't refuse Daniel even if constant exposure to his presence increased her own pain.

"I have the time," Abby said quietly. "I'm flattered you want my help with the house."

"We're more alike than you know, so I trust whatever you'll do with it."

We're more alike than you know.

Abby ran a hand through her hair. A few minutes with Daniel was all it took to reduce her insides to slush.

"It would be nice if you could have final approval on carpeting and curtains, though," she said. "They are like permanent fixtures in the house and you must like what you get. It might be easier for you to work with an interior-decorating firm in Los Angeles."

That would save her the pain of having to meet him over and over again.

Daniel looked surprised. "We can choose the curtains and carpets right here. Once escrow goes through on the house, I plan on spending all my weekends here. Sarah has offered me the use of the guest house till the house is ready to move into."

Abby couldn't suppress the spurt of irritation she felt. Gran never made anything easier.

"Are you in a hurry to get back?" Daniel asked as Abby picked up her bag and dusted it off.

"N... not really. I have an appointment with Mrs. G. at seven."

"It's only six. I won't keep you long. I want to show you something we didn't have time for the other day." Daniel unlocked and opened the patio door.

Abby stepped outside. Two paths curved from the patio through a vast expanse of carefully cared-for grass and trees. Daniel chose the one that disappeared to the rear of the yard. "This way."

The path led past a carefully laid-out kitchen garden, now bare except for some overgrown herbs, and a little rock garden. Where it stopped, the land sloped gently upward for fifty yards. Steps made with railroad ties added to the charm of the natural surroundings.

She wasn't quite sure whether it was the climb or the fact that halfway up Daniel had cupped her elbow that made her so breathless.

At the top of the steps, Daniel put an arm around Abby's shoulders. Quivering, she stepped away from his side and looked around. Her willpower was in danger of being shot to pieces. Below her she could see the rest of the city. All around towered the sides of the canyons that had given Carbon Canyon its name.

"Look behind you."

Abby turned and her breath caught in her throat. The sun was a sinking ball of vermilion, and the clouds in the sky reflected shades of color that defied the imagination of any human artist. Abby looked at the bare walls of the canyon. They seemed to be plated with copper.

"It's beautiful." Abby wished words weren't so inadequate to express what she felt.

"I climbed up here the first time I saw the house. As I stood and watched the sun go down, I felt I belonged here."

Abby kept quiet. There was no reason for the place to tug at *her* heart this way.

The first time he'd seen the place Daniel had realized he wanted the house for all it represented. Home, wife, children.

Staying in Carbon Canyon he'd admitted work only filled emptiness temporarily. Family alone did a permanent job.

"It's the first time I've felt like this about a place since my parents died."

Abby swallowed. More than anything, Daniel needed a place where he could put down roots.

"It's how I feel about us as well, Abby. That we belong together."

Abby turned to look at him as the color drained from her face.

The wind whipped her hair across her face. Daniel lifted one hand to move the strand caught in her lips aside. "All I'm asking is that you give both of us a chance to let our feelings develop."

His gaze turned back to the sunset and it was hard to read his expression. He'd said the words so casually, Abby wondered what Daniel had in mind. An affair? She couldn't afford to indulge in one.

Abby glanced at him. He seemed absorbed in the sky. In Daniel's world, there was probably nothing wrong in making these decisions in a businesslike manner. He and his fiancée had lived together, then discovered they had very little in common and broken their engagement.

The old Abby might have accepted his offer, but the last few weeks had changed her life. The new Abby believed in her power to give one-hundred percent in the right relationship. Her self-esteem insisted she accept nothing less in return. She wanted more than a business arrangement.

Which left her with only one choice. Abby looked at the walls of the canyon. Like her thoughts, they were dark and cold. The sun had set.

"I can't afford to experiment." Her throat ached with the effort to sound calm.

Daniel turned to her. He had hardly dared to breathe these last few minutes. Giving her time to think things through, accept what he was leading up to, had been hard. Only Abby hadn't been thinking about accepting anything. She'd been framing a refusal.

"Are you scared that what we have might not last?"

Abby shook her head. The words tumbling in her mind, couldn't be said.

I'm scared that if I fail again, I won't be able to put myself back together.

"I'll see you back at the house." She turned away before he saw the tears in her eyes.

Daniel sighed. Telling Abby he wanted to marry her, was a challenge he hadn't figured out how to deal with.

Stop postponing the discussion, Hawthorn.

In his seminars, he'd always said timing was important in business. Every business move he'd ever made had a ninety-five percent chance of success attached to it.

Timing was even more important with Abby. With her, he just couldn't predict his chances of success. One minute her kisses were driving him crazy, the next she was treating him as if he were a stranger. Daniel knew marriage scared her. She'd told him so herself. Caution warned to let the matter drop. Intuition pointed out he'd made a mess of everything by being indirect.

"Abby, I have something to ask you." He caught her arm, stopping her headlong rush back to the drive. Maybe the only mistake he was making with her was being too careful. Spontaneity might work better than anything else ever had.

"Yes?"

She turned to look at him and Daniel said in a rush, "Abby, would you like to live in this house with me?"

The pounding of her heart convinced Abby she had been right all along. This close to him she could see how hard he was breathing. His eyes bored into the depths of her mind.

Abby stepped back and ran a hand through her hair. Daniel's suggestion they live together wasn't such a bad idea. In fact, it was considered quite normal these days for people in love. Only Daniel hadn't mentioned love.

Her gaze dropped to his mouth.

Recalling what he had said once about the careful evaluation of a project, as well as a woman, Abby felt this must be another business deal for Daniel.

She was available. She wasn't a demanding type like Eve had been. It would be a very convenient arrangement.

"No."

Emotion pulsing in her throat wouldn't allow her to elaborate. Pain, frustration, *rage*. Daniel had forgotten one thing. She wasn't the type for such a cold-blooded arrangement. Abby wished she had never set eyes on Daniel Hawthorn. Wished he hadn't brought her heart out of cold storage. Hurting, she turned away.

The abruptness of Abby's reply startled Daniel. She hadn't taken very long to consider what he'd said. He'd meant to lead up to the subject of marriage, but there was no point in it now. If there was one thing Abby knew, it was her own mind. To sound so definite, she must have thought about the subject and decided she didn't care for him after all.

"I'm sorry I suggested it," he said stiffly.

The timing wasn't right. Probably, Daniel admitted, looking at Abby's averted face, it would never be.

Later that night, Abby sat on the window seat, glad the day had finally come to an end. She had to sort out her thoughts. The urge to buy herself a box of chocolates had been very strong, but Abby had managed to avoid it.

Deciding she wasn't the type for an affair left her with only one startling option. Marriage.

It was time to stop running and face her fears.

Marriage was a partnership. If either partner did not bring their full one-hundred percent to it, it would never work. With Rod, she had given increasingly more, but it hadn't been enough. Over the last few weeks she'd finally realized the marriage had failed because Rod hadn't wanted to give anything.

It hadn't been her fault.

The knowledge had freed Abby from the heavy burden of guilt she had carried around for so long. Around Daniel, a new hope had begun to sprout. That she would have a second chance to try love again.

Why had he stamped it out?

The answer hurt. Daniel was honest enough to admit he wanted a relationship. She ought to appreciate the fact he hadn't offered any false promises. Abby supposed if she considered Daniel's suggestion calmly, she would see it was a modern arrangement.

Only she wasn't a modern woman. Not in that sense of the word. Gran and Gramps had raised her with values she couldn't discard at a moment's notice. Now her own self-esteem wouldn't let her accept anything less than what she wanted out of life.

She wasn't interested in down to earth. Not in this aspect of her life. Abby preferred having nothing, if she couldn't have moonlight and magic, tender promises and shared dreams. The fact love hadn't come her way didn't mean it didn't exist. Abby wanted all the things that went hand in hand with loving someone.

All the things that were out of her reach.

"I'm going to New York tomorrow to meet with my editor," Daniel told Sarah later that day. "You don't need my help around here anymore. I'll be back to collect my things at the end of the week, if you don't mind."

Maybe a week would make Abby change her mind.

"Of course I don't mind," Sarah said. "Leave Princess with us. She'll miss you, but being here will be better for her than being in a kennel in Los Angeles."

"Are you sure?" Daniel was hesitant to impose on them.

"Of course. And Daniel . . . ?"

"Yes?"

"The fact we don't *need* your help anymore doesn't mean we don't *want* you around. You'll always be welcome here. Now, what shall I tell Abby?"

Daniel had no message for Abby. "I'll be back by the end of the week."

"Right. Do you need any help packing?"

"No, thanks." He could do that himself. What it seemed he couldn't do himself was figure out Abby.

Beside him, he heard Sarah sigh. "You're a good man, Daniel. Just like my David. You'll find a way to get through to that granddaughter of mine."

"I thought so until yesterday," said Daniel. "Now, I don't know anymore."

"Sometimes I think it's my fault. David and I brought Abby up to believe in marriage and happily-ever-after. That's one reason she married so young. She tried so hard to make it work. For a time she blamed herself for the fact things didn't work out."

"I know."

"To reach out again to something that's hurt you once takes tremendous courage."

Daniel simply nodded. He couldn't tell Sarah that her granddaughter had decided never to try marriage again.

Chapter Eleven

Abby thought of Daniel all day. Looking back she realized two things about their discussion. Every deal, business or otherwise, had two parties. Both stated their needs before an agreement was reached.

In their case, it hadn't worked that way. Daniel had suggested they get to know each other better. He had asked her if she would like to live in the house with him. Instead of telling him what *she* wanted, Abby had jumped to her own conclusions, reacted like a heroine in a Gothic novel and had a fit of the vapors.

Daniel had wanted to discuss the matter further, but she hadn't let him. She hadn't given him a reason for her behavior. Did the fact he hadn't asked for one mean he wasn't really interested?

Had she lost him? The thought scared Abby more than anything else in the world.

If buying herself protection against pain meant paying with loneliness, she didn't want any of that kind of insurance. Taking a chance with Daniel, even if he might discover he didn't feel anything for her, was better than existing in the emotional vacuum she had taken up residence in these past few years.

She had to talk to him, find the courage to tell him what she wanted out of the arrangement.

Knocking on the door of the guest house mid-afternoon, Abby realized Daniel's car wasn't in the carport. Was he out? Reluctant to leave when she had just mustered up all her courage to get to this point, Abby decided to go in and write Daniel a note. He never locked the door. Turning the doorknob, Abby pushed it open.

Her heart sank as she took in the sight of the empty rooms. Every trace of Daniel's presence had vanished. Only the scent of the lemony after-shave he used hung tauntingly in the air.

She had never felt so alone in her life. Abby ran a hand through her hair. She was too late.

"Gran?" Abby turned around, as Sarah entered the guest house with an armful of clean towels. "When did Daniel leave?"

"A little while back, but he left Princess here."

As much as Abby liked Princess, the dog was no substitute for her owner.

"He said he'd be back when his business in New York is finished."

"I see." Taking the clean towels from Gran, Abby put them away in the chest of drawers.

"He's left a contact number where we can reach him."

The ball was definitely in her court. Abby hesitated. What could she say? *Daniel, come back. I've decided to give our feelings a try. Daniel, I made a mistake. Give me another chance.*

Abby shook her head. "Thanks Gran. I'll think about it."

She went into the community room. Maybe some whittling would help calm her down. Abby looked at her shelf and her eyes narrowed. There was a brown paper parcel there with her name on it.

Abby reached for it and unwrapped it. There was something vaguely familiar about the shape.

Tears filled her eyes when she saw the odd-shaped bird Daniel had worked on the past few weeks. Sanded and varnished with black beads for eyes, it looked more like a pregnant frog than a bird. Abby hugged it to her. Daniel couldn't have given her anything she liked more.

Losing Daniel was like a knife in her heart. She had no one but herself to blame. She had taken too long mustering her courage. And Daniel, as she'd known right from the start, was not a patient man.

Her fingers brushed against a piece of paper fixed to the frog's underside. Turning it over, Abby peeled off the tape that held the paper in place.

Beauty lies in the eyes of the beholder.

Daniel's message reminded her of his insistence that she was beautiful. She had batted away his compliments, refused to believe in them. She had run away from what was important one too many times.

"Men don't always find it easy to express their feelings. They wait to get a sign from a woman. They almost have to be assured they won't be refused before they'll propose. It has something to do with our egos."

Abby turned to Hamish. How long had he been there? She got the message loud and clear. Daniel was a prince, and she was the fool who had refused to wake up when he had kissed her.

"A man who's been turned down once is worse than all the rest," Hamish continued. "He would almost need to be hit over the head with encouragement."

Daniel had talked of signals once, too. Hope was a tiny ember in Abby's heart. Had she sent the wrong signals?

Going into the office, Abby sat down, still holding Daniel's gift. Gathering her courage, finding Daniel and telling him she would be willing to explore their new relationship, wouldn't be easy. She had to be strong enough to realize that it might not amount to anything. Tough enough to withstand the pain that would result.

Would it be worth the risk?

We are what we choose to believe we are, Abby.

Daniel's words challenged her. What did she believe she was?

"I'm a survivor."

Abby heard herself saying the words aloud. They were true. She'd survived a bad marriage, found the courage to put the pieces of her life back together. Now she had decided that no matter what, she had to risk everything again.

The alternative—being a spectator not a participant, watching life go by—was no fun at all. Besides, she wasn't the only one in the world who'd experienced pain and grief and failure. Some people had to build only once in life, others had to keep rebuilding. The only failures were those who gave up.

Abby lifted her head. She'd finally found the courage she needed. Now it was a matter of finding the number Daniel had left. She'd call him first thing in the morning.

Her eyes narrowed as she caught sight of the large white envelope on the table. Gran had printed her name on it. Curious, Abby opened the envelope. It was a ticket to the Hot Tub Resort in Carbon Canyon. There was a note with it.

For Abby, Gran had printed. Thank you for all you've done for us.

They had discovered the resort last summer. Gran had sprained her knee and Dr. Davisson had advised her soaking in a hot tub would help. He'd mentioned the new resort next to the Carbon Canyon golf course. Gran and Abby had visited the place quite a few times.

Set in the hillside at the resort were nine spas. Each was enclosed on three sides to ensure complete privacy, while the glass on the fourth side allowed a one-hundred-and-eighty-degree view of the city below. At night, the view was spectacular.

Abby looked at the time on her reservation card. Seven o'clock. It would be perfect to sit in the bubbling water in the dark and let it soak some of the confusion out of her. The trio had been invited to a country dance competition organized by a local church. She'd have to go to the hot tub resort alone. It was better than sitting home and worrying over what to say to Daniel.

Exactly at seven Abby pulled up outside the Hot Tub Resort.

"Here's to some rest and relaxation," Abby told herself wryly, as she stepped out of the car.

She had a swimsuit on under the green-and-white towelling robe Agnes had made for her. Patterned on a housedress, the coverup tied at the neck and had a pocket at the side. Abby had noticed how her new eating habits improved her silhouette. She'd never looked so good in this swimsuit before.

Her hair was knotted on top of her head, secured with a couple of pins so it wouldn't get wet. Picking up the bag that held her change of clothes, Abby locked the car. She was all set.

Shrugging off the loneliness that had clamped down on her, Abby headed for the office.

The woman inside smiled when Abby showed her the ticket. "Straight down the path and then turn to your left. The number is painted on the back of each building. You can't miss it."

Abby wondered why the woman hadn't shown her to the hot tub. Someone had always escorted Gran and herself to the tubs on previous visits. Not that it really mattered. She knew where number seven was.

Opening the door, Abby put a hand out to the light switch.

"Hi, Abby!"

The velvety voice turned her blood to ice. Gran and Gramps had taught her prayers were always answered. Abby hadn't expected hers being anticipated.

"Daniel."

Her heart defied medical history and missed a beat. She looked at him. That half smile was in place. The dark eyes looked at her with the old, familiar intensity.

"The trio have been busy."

It explained their strange behavior earlier. "Did you get a ticket, too?"

Daniel nodded. "It was in the guest house. I know the trio too well to know it wasn't a plain thank-you gift. I hoped it would be something like this."

Abby felt she couldn't breathe. She had to make good use of this opportunity.

"I was going to call you tomorrow. I wanted to talk with you, tell you how wrong I was...."

Her voice trailed away as her thoughts became muddled. The foaming water around him accentuated Daniel's big, bare chest. She wanted to touch him, reassure herself he really was back.

"Close the door, Abby," invited Daniel, reaching for the ice chest beside the tub and pouring wine into two flutes. "What were you wrong about?"

It was so good to see her again. He couldn't wait to see what she had on under the dress.

Daniel's gaze made her feel weak. Sitting down on the edge of the tub, Abby slipped her feet into the water. Her gaze lifted to his mouth, and her mind went blank.

"I shouldn't have been so abrupt about your suggestion at the new house." Abby wet her lips and swallowed the lump in her throat. Challenging Daniel at his seminar seemed easy compared to this. "What I mean is, in your line of work, you're used to approaching situations in a businesslike way. This is no different."

Abby closed her eyes for a second. The urge to get up and run was very strong.

Daniel's eyes widened. What on earth did Abby mean? How could love and the rest of one's life be compared to a business proposition?

You gave her that impression that day up at the house, Hawthorn, you tongue-tied fool.

He had never felt so lonely and empty as he had after he'd decided to leave Carbon Canyon. The thought of returning to a way of life that held no appeal had stopped him. He'd known he had to find Abby and tell her how he felt in plain, simple English. He loved her.

Daniel's gaze meshed with Abby's. He knew he had to be very careful rewinding whatever had happened between them, and starting all over again.

"Why were you going to call me, Abby?"

"No reason." She felt like a lump of wet clay. Daniel didn't seem interested in discussing what had happened at his house.

"Abby." He didn't say anything more. He didn't have to. The word was a warning. He had reached the end of his patience.

Abby knew she had to come up with an explanation Daniel would believe. "I wanted to apologize for comparing you to...to anyone else that night at the house. It wasn't fair of me."

"Thank you, Abby. Now, come into the water."

Abby stared at him. That was it? No recriminations, no lengthy sermons? Just come into the water?

The water sloshed around Daniel as he moved to get the wine flutes and hand her one.

"Is that the only reason you wanted to call?" Daniel asked, when she didn't move.

"Yes." She couldn't help sounding defensive. His look turned her willpower to mush. It wasn't fair.

Daniel shook his head. "I was hoping you'd say you called to tell me you care about me as much as I care about you."

The room tilted around her. Had she heard right?

"We're from different worlds."

The protest sounded halfhearted. Abby wanted to buy herself some time, make sure this wasn't a scene she was imagining.

When had Daniel moved closer? His hand was on one ankle and he was gently massaging her foot. The exquisite sensation fogged her mind.

"I know we're from different worlds. That's what makes it so interesting."

She couldn't keep the truth back any longer. "I can't move in with you."

"What?"

The way Daniel yelled the word scared Abby, but she went on. "That last day at the house . . . you suggested we live together for a while, find out if we're right for each other."

Daniel felt the tension go out of his muscles. He'd been right about making one big mess of everything.

"And you're not willing to do that?"

"Well . . . Gran says sometimes half a loaf is better than no bread, but I don't agree. I love you so much, I can't accept half a loaf."

Abby felt herself blush. She hadn't intended to blurt everything out like that.

"And that's what you think I'm offering you? Half a loaf?"

"Isn't it?"

"When I asked you to live with me in the house, I had marriage in mind."

"M . . . marriage," Abby stammered. Daniel's hand caressed the arch of her foot. The sensation lit a fire in the pit of Abby's stomach.

Daniel held a hand up. "Let me finish. I know marriage scares you because of what happened to you the first time around. I thought if I asked you to marry me outright you would refuse. So I took you to see the house, hoping it would help change your mind."

"Marriage," Abby repeated in a daze.

Daniel reached for her hands. "That's why I'm buying the house. It's for you, our children, maybe even our grandchildren one day. I know now that a man can have every material possession in the world, but if he doesn't have love, he has nothing."

Abby stared at him. She wasn't going to interrupt this time around.

"I love you too much to settle for half a loaf," Daniel said.

"Oh."

Abby's thoughts wandered. Daniel's hands were busy untying the ribbon at the neck of her robe.

"I want forever with you Abby."

She couldn't say a word. Abby's gaze clung to Daniel's and in his eyes she read the promise of their future together.

There was something she had to say. "Happily-ever-after doesn't really exist outside fairy tales."

"Results equal effort, determination and persistence," Daniel retorted. It sounded like a line from his seminar. "Happily-ever-after is up to us."

There was nothing she could say to that.

"Abby..." Daniel's hand slid down her shoulder and arm, coming to rest on her thigh. "Are you going to spend all our time here talking?"

"You don't want to talk?"

"No," said Daniel. "Remember what you told me once? Actions speak louder than words. I know you want to go slow, but I'm done with slow. I tried it and it didn't work. I almost lost you. I'm going to try it my way now."

"Which is?"

"Come into the water and let me prove I love you."

Her phantom fears that he might not care as much as she did vanished forever. The pulse beating erratically in Abby's throat erupted into a wild tango.

"Abby." There was unmistakable command in Daniel's voice as he set his glass down and held both hands out to her.

Standing up, Abby suddenly felt shy. Putting a hand out she switched off the light.

"Daniel," she asked, nervously tugging her robe over her head, "are you wearing a swimsuit?"

He smiled, moving away from her to the opposite side so he could look at her. The moonlight streaming in through the glass gave him plenty of light to see by. He took his time completing his survey, glad that Abby made no move to hide herself as she would have a few weeks ago.

"You're beautiful Abby." She couldn't doubt the note of sincerity in Daniel's voice. He meant every word of what he said. "About your question . . . ?"

"Yes?" said Abby, tearing her eyes away from the strong column of his neck with difficulty. What had her question been?

The smile on Daniel's face made her heart pound. "I have one of my own to ask first. When will you marry me?"

She liked the way he phrased it. Not will you marry me, but *when* will you? He really had forgiven her for putting them through some unnecessary misery.

"Soon," said Abby.

"Would you mind being married at the new house?"

Abby shook her head. It would be a perfect setting for their beginning.

"I promise to do my best to make you happy."

"We'll both do our best," Abby corrected gently. Daniel's words handed her a licence to dream, to believe, to be happy. "Marriage is a joint venture."

"About your question . . ." said Daniel.

"Which one?" Abby asked dreamily.

"You'll have to come in and find out if I'm wearing anything or not," he said smoothly.

Abby slid into the water and into Daniel's waiting arms. He gathered her to his chest and kissed her hungrily. Wrapping her arms around him, Abby responded passionately. Her hands skimmed the sides of his body, pausing as they rested on his briefs.

"Oh," she said, as Daniel lifted his head.

"I know," he said, a tinge of regret in his voice. "But there's Sarah and the others to think of. They'll make a formidable set of in-laws as it is, and I don't want to upset them by not respecting their feelings."

Trust Daniel to think of everything. Abby pressed her lips against the strong column of Daniel's neck. "Thank you."

Daniel couldn't resist teasing Abby. "Besides, you've taught me there's a great deal to be said for doing some things the old-fashioned way."

"I have?" Abby asked, as she nibbled on Daniel's ear. His reaction was very satisfying. They could talk later.

The pressure of his mouth on her neck and the touch of his hands repeated all the assurances of his love. Abby knew Daniel and she would face the challenge of life together. They would keep some of the old-fashioned ways of doing things, mix it with the new, to produce the best results.

"Kiss me, Abby."

Daniel's voice was husky with need. Pushing her thoughts aside, Abby concentrated on enjoying the moment. As Daniel had said, the time for words was past. It was time for action.

*   *   *   *   *

**HE'S MORE THAN
A MAN, HE'S
ONE OF OUR**

UNCLE DADDY

Kasey Michaels

Gabe Logan was doing just fine raising his orphaned niece
alone. He didn't need or *want* any help from the baby's aunt,
Erica Fletcher. Gabe could see that the uptight businesswoman
didn't have a clue about child rearing. So when Erica
suggested Gabe teach her about parenting, it was an offer he
couldn't resist. Having her move into his house would surely
force Erica to admit defeat. But when she set out to conquer his
heart...Gabe knew he was in big trouble!

Find out the true meaning of *close quarters* in Kasey Michaels's
UNCLE DADDY, available in February.

Fall in love with our **Fabulous Fathers**—and join the Silhouette
Romance family!

ROMANCE™

**Three All-American beauties discover
love comes in all shapes and sizes!**

ALL-AMERICAN SWEETHEARTS

by Laurie Paige

CARA'S BELOVED (#917)—*February*

SALLY'S BEAU (#923)—*March*

VICTORIA'S CONQUEST (#933)—*April*

A lost love, a new love and a hidden one, three
All-American Sweethearts get their men in Paradise Falls,
West Virginia. Only in America . . . and only
from Silhouette Romance!

Silhouette
R O M A N C E™

SMYTHESHIRE, MASSACHUSETTS.

Small town. Big secrets.

Silhouette Romance invites you to visit Elizabeth August's small town, a place with a legacy rooted deep in the past....

THE VIRGIN WIFE
February 1993
Madaline MacGreggor-Smythe lived a far-from-ordinary existence. Though married, she had never experienced romantic intimacy and probably never would. But when Colin Darnell—a man from Madaline's past—returns to town, feelings long denied are rekindled. And so is the danger that had separated them!

HAUNTED HUSBAND
March 1993—FABULOUS FATHERS
Thatcher Brant, widower and father of two, vowed never to love again. This chief of police would not risk his feelings, or those of his children, for anyone. Least of all, Samantha Hogan. But *something* had told Samantha that Thatcher was the husband for her!

SMYTHESHIRE, MASSACHUSETTS—this sleepy little town has plenty to keep you up at night. Only from Silhouette Romance!

Silhouette
R O M A N C E™

get
Steph
Pearson

Silhouette
ROMANCE™

HEARTLAND
HOLIDAYS

Christmas bells turn into wedding bells for the Gallagher siblings in Stella Bagwell's *Heartland Holidays* trilogy.

THEIR FIRST THANKSGIVING (#903) in November
Olivia Westcott had once rejected Sam Gallagher's proposal—and in his stubborn pride, he'd refused to hear her reasons why. Now Olivia is back...and it is about time Sam Gallagher listened!

THE BEST CHRISTMAS EVER (#909) in December
Soldier Nick Gallagher had come home to be the best man at his brother's wedding—not to be a groom! But when he met single mother Allison Lee, he knew he'd found his bride.

NEW YEAR'S BABY (#915) in January
Kathleen Gallagher had given up on love and marriage until she came to the rescue of neighbor Ross Douglas...and the newborn baby he'd found on his doorstep!

Come celebrate the holidays with Silhouette Romance!
